2 Days

L.B. Tillit

SADDLEBACK
EDUCATIONAL PUBLISHING

GRAVEL ROAD

SADDLEBACK
EDUCATIONAL PUBLISHING
www.sdlback.com

Copyright ©2012 by Saddleback Educational Publishing

ISBN-13: 978-1-61651-793-9
ISBN-10: 1-61651-793-X
eBook: 978-1-61247-383-3

Printed in Guangzhou, China
NOR/0616/CA21601119

20 19 18 17 16   2 3 4 5 6

Gravel Road

ACKNOWLEDGMENTS

I would like to thank the Public Health Department and Sheila Gardin-Mooney for sharing their knowledge concerning teen pregnancy. I would like to thank my children, Sarah, Amy, and Maya, my husband, Tore, and my family for their unending support. Additional thanks to Anne Wanicka, my mentor and friend.

My greatest gratitude goes to my students whose true stories remain more unbelievable than fiction. They are my heroes.

CHAPTER 1

New Year's Day

Get out!" Mom yelled at me as I grabbed my warmest fleece jacket from the closet. "How dare you accuse De Monte." I couldn't believe Mom was choosing her boyfriend over me. I was sixteen, not some little kid telling stories. I knew it was wrong for De Monte to touch my breasts. I knew it wasn't an accident. It wasn't the first time. I knew he was a creep when he was drunk. But that didn't mean he could do what he wanted. How could Mom not see this? How could she believe him and not her own daughter?

"Mom, please!" I begged as I pulled the jacket over my shaking arms. "He's lying. Don't do this!"

When she didn't answer me, I ran into my room. But Mom followed me. She was not letting up. "Neema, I said get out!"

"Mom!" I yelled back. "I'm going." I could feel tears flowing down my cheeks. I looked her right in the eyes.

"You have to let me take some of my stuff. I can't go without anything." Mom turned and stomped out the door. I tried to calm myself and take a deep breath. I had to pull myself together.

The room I had called mine for three years had a window that looked out over Pine Street. It was usually a busy street. But everything was dead that day. It was January first. I could see a few flurries and knew my jacket wouldn't be enough. I was already shaking, and I hadn't even stepped outside yet. I walked over to my bed and touched the red and blue quilt that Mom had given me. She said she got it from her mother. It would be perfect to keep out the cold.

I grabbed the quilt off my bed and shoved it under one arm while I grabbed my overstuffed, yellow handbag in the other. I glanced inside the bag. I had my phone and my wallet, along with lip gloss and other random things like eyeliner, a bottle of Tylenol, a couple of CDs I burned myself, and some tampons. I thought they were emergency items at the time. I was suddenly scrambling for real emergency items.

I could hear Mom and De Monte cussing in the other room. I told myself I needed to clear my head. Think, Neema! Think! I had to make sure I had enough for a few days. I shoved underwear and a pair of blue jeans in the bag. I looked at the closet full of clothes. There were new ones and those I had kept for memory's sake. I had to leave them.

I looked at the pile of stuffed animals and old dolls that sat neatly on my dressers. I had to leave them too. I looked at the pictures neatly stuck to my wall. One of my mother and me smiling. A few of me pretending to be a top model. Then there was a single picture of my father in uniform. He looked about twenty. I never knew him. I believed he was saving the world. I ripped all the photos from the wall and stuffed them into my bag.

I took a glance in the mirror. I looked awful. My hair was all crazy. I hadn't even washed my face. I hadn't had time to get ready to go out. I never would have left my home like this. I was always the best-looking girl at school. Always hair with the newest style. Always makeup to show off my beautiful brown eyes. The girls always said I looked like Beyoncé, with beautiful caramel skin and a body others would kill for. But at that moment I looked like a mess.

I suddenly felt De Monte towering over me. I turned to face him. "You heard your mother. Get out!" His angry, black face was looking down at me. I could still smell the stink of his partying from the night before. The night he tried to touch my Beyoncé body.

"Get away from me, creep!" I moved away from him and headed toward the door. He followed. Mom was standing in the kitchen crying. Black eyeliner was smeared across her smooth, brown cheeks. She wouldn't even look at me. I wasn't sure if she was crying for herself or me.

"Mom?" I begged one more time. She didn't even look at me. My own mother let me walk down the steps to the outside door and stand on the cold street. I knew she was crying for herself.

I stood for a few minutes in front of De Monte's Pawn Shop. He'd moved us to his upstairs apartment when Mom needed a place for us to live. He'd been good when I was younger. But booze and time had changed him.

The snow started to come down a little harder. I awkwardly carried my belongings toward the subway station. There was no way I would be out in the cold for long. I had money to get on the next ride to Park Central Station. Only two stops away. I took out my phone. My hands were shaking. I texted Nate that I was on my way. He'd been my boyfriend for six months. I knew he would help me.

As I sat in the warmth of the subway car, I finally let myself breathe. I wish I hadn't. I wish I'd stayed on running mode. But I didn't. Suddenly I was crying again. There were only four other people sitting nearby. They didn't even turn their heads. They didn't care. So I didn't care. I just cried.

CHAPTER 2

Shelter

The snow had stopped when I got off at Park Central. There were tall trees surrounding a park where some kids were playing. The snowfall had not given much to play with, but the kids were excited anyway. I walked to one of the four apartment buildings that surrounded the park like a large fortress. I found the right door and pushed the doorbell that read Boyd. My heart raced. I hoped they would be home. It was noon. Nate hadn't answered my text. I pulled out my phone and texted again. This time I got a response. "I'm not home. Wait for me at the park. I'll come get you. Got a car." Car? I found that strange. Exciting too! Thinking about the car took my mind off of Mom. I pushed away her words. I pushed her away.

I walked over to the kids again and sat down on a wet bench. I covered myself with my quilt. It brought some warmth. I waited half an hour before Nate pulled up in an old, blue Chevy station wagon. His window was rolled down, and I could see the smooth, brown skin of his arm facing the cold. Nate looked like he was on a summer afternoon drive with just a T-shirt on. His hair was in tight cornrows, and he smiled a smile that would make any girl melt. He parked and got out of the car.

"Dang, you look like an old bag lady." Nate laughed as he walked up to me. I looked at him and started to cry again. He sat down next to me and crawled under the quilt. "Come on, baby. It can't be that bad. Tell me what's going on."

So I told him.

Nate was quiet at first. Then he asked me, "Do you want me to beat up De Monte?"

I smiled and told him, "That won't help Mom any. But it's a sweet thought." I sighed and added, "I just need a place to crash until I can figure out what to do next."

Nate stood up and grabbed my purse for me. "Come on. Let me take you for a ride."

"In that?" I said with disgust as I pointed at the station wagon.

He laughed. "You should be talking! Have you seen yourself?"

I stuck out my tongue and followed him. Once I was sitting next him in the wide front seat that let me slide up close I asked, "Where'd you get this piece of junk?"

Nate laughed. "Guy down the street sold it to me for two hundred cash. Said he needed the money bad." I frowned. He glanced at me a minute. "Don't worry I'm going to use it down at the shop. The guys and I are going to use its parts or I may turn it into something amazing myself." I rolled my eyes. I couldn't quite see a pimped-up Chevy station wagon. "You'll see." He smiled and reached over and touched my leg.

His warmth made me relax. I leaned my head against his shoulder as we spent the day riding around in his car. By evening Nate parked in a dark spot near his apartment. I spread my quilt out in the back. The seats went down and made a huge space. We giggled and snuggled. One thing led to another. It wasn't my first time with Nate. In fact, it was part of who we were as a couple. In fact, it was all we were as a couple.

Nate invited me to stay with his family until I could work things out with Mom. Mr. and Mrs. Boyd weren't too happy with Nate bringing me home. He had two younger brothers that shared a room with him. This meant I got the couch. But Mrs. Boyd smiled the best she could. I could stay. But only a few days.

It was Wednesday. School started Monday. I told myself that not much could happen in a few days.

CHAPTER 3

Emergency Item

Crap!" I shuffled through my bag. I had a towel wrapped around me. The morning shower had felt good. But my relaxed feeling was leaving me. I was in a panic. The bathroom was small, so the pile of objects I was pulling out of my bag started to look like a small mountain on the tiled floor. I stood still looking at my emergency items. Why I didn't think of my birth control pills is beyond me.

I slowly picked up my clean underwear, jeans, and T-shirt and got dressed. I would give Mom a couple of days to calm down, and I would swing by to pick up a few items. Like my pills. A couple of days couldn't hurt. At least that's what I told myself. I was so wrong!

CHAPTER 4

Quick Fix

I've got to run by and see if I can get in the house." I was snuggled up against Nate. I was getting used to the old-car smell. I had spent the last two days listening to his ideas of how he would fix up the car. It was clear he wasn't going to break it down for parts. Talking about the car meant I didn't have to talk about Mom or De Monte. At first I wished Nate had asked me more, but he didn't. I told myself this was good. Now I dreaded bringing it up again.

"What for?" he asked as he turned a corner. We were a block away from Pine Street.

"Got to get a couple of things I forgot," I said, trying to make it sound like no big deal. Even though it had been two days, I figured if I grabbed the pills and took one I'd be okay. I didn't need to worry Nate.

"You think it's a good idea?" He sounded worried.

"If I'm right, De Monte will have his pawn shop open today, and Mom will be working at the beauty shop." I smiled for a moment remembering Mom trying out new hairstyles on me before she showed them to her customers. I was the envy of all the girls. She may not have made much money, but she made her baby girl look good. I pushed away the lump in my throat. I would not cry.

"Okay, but be careful." Nate pulled up slowly. The pawn shop sign was flickering on and off. He was too cheap to get it fixed. I looked out my window and saw De Monte behind the counter. He was shaking his head at an old man who was holding a vacuum.

"Good! He's busy." I smiled at Nate. He pulled around to the side of the building. It was a small alleyway with enough room for me to hop out. I grabbed my empty bag and ran up the stairs. I opened the door using my own key. I stopped for just a minute. The apartment was quiet, and the smell of home made me want to give in to my tears. I pushed them away again. I had to focus.

I ran into the small bathroom next to my room. I found the pills still neatly packaged. Small arrows pointed from one pill to the next. I stared at the two I'd missed. I pushed the first one through the wrapping and swallowed it. I shoved the rest of the pills in my bag.

I went into my room and grabbed a couple of my best jeans, some pretty tops, and my newest shoes. My favorite earrings were in a small box next to my bed, so I grabbed them too. I had to go to school the next day and wanted to look good.

I suddenly heard the door slam. My heart raced. I ran out of my room to find De Monte standing between me and the door. He was breathing hard. "What are you doing here?"

I held up my bag. "Had to get a few things." I tried to sound calm. But I could tell he saw my fear.

He walked up to me. "So you think you can break into my home and get away with it."

"I didn't break in." I held up my key. "This is my stuff." I was starting to shake.

He moved in close and looked me in the eye. I could feel his breath on my face. He'd been drinking again. I tried to stare back. But I looked away. I started to move around him when he reached for me. I hit his hand away before he could touch me. I dropped the key on the floor.

He cussed and was about to hit me when the door opened. "Are you ready to go?" Nate's eyes were big. He didn't look at De Monte right away. He didn't want to challenge him. He knew De Monte would win. He finally looked up at the towering man. Nate smiled, "Hey, De Monte. What's up?"

De Monte nodded and didn't know quite what to say. So he grunted.

"Hear the shop's doing well." Nate was looking at De

Monte. But his arms were reaching for me. He was waving for me to head out the door.

I didn't wait. I ran. All I could hear was Nate yelling, "Good talking to you."

We jumped in the car. Nate drove away fast. We didn't speak until we reached an old parking lot that had belonged to a store. The store was gone, but the concrete was still there. Small tufts of grass were trying to push through and reclaim the space.

"Thanks," I whispered. I looked at Nate. I finally gave in to the tears. He pulled me close. I felt so safe. He kissed me. I kissed back. Soon we both didn't care if it was in the middle of the afternoon or not.

I thought for only a moment about the missed pills. Only for a moment. I had no idea that two missed days could make such a huge difference in my life.

CHAPTER 5

Back to School

Monday finally came. I cleaned myself up nicely and walked into the second semester of my junior year acting like nothing had happened. Nate held my hand and met me in the hall between classes. He was a senior, but we still had time together at school.

"So you moved in with Nate?" Tia pulled her desk as close as possible. English was about to begin, but Mr. Ray hadn't showed up yet.

"What's up with that?" Rose came at me from the other side. Rose and Tia had been my best friends since third grade. The teacher would always mix us up. She never could remember who was who. So we'd start really messing with the teacher by wearing the same clothes and wearing the same hair styles. But once we hit middle school, there was no problem telling us apart. Rose gained twenty pounds, mostly in her butt. Tia grew ten inches and colored her hair red. We learned to jump rope together, dance together, have crushes on boys together, and finally party together. But we kept the partying as far away from our parents as possible. Tia, Rose, and I were close. I could tell them anything.

"Mom kicked me out," I whispered. At this point I didn't feel like crying anymore. I told myself I could do this. I could live without Mom.

"No way!" Rose covered her mouth. Then she frowned. "Why didn't you call me?"

"Or me?" Tia slapped my arm gently. "You know you could always crash with me."

"I know." I smiled. "But Nate was the first to come to my mind."

"Oooh!" Rose teased. "He keeping you warm?"

"You know he is," I teased back.

"Well, I can't compete with that," Tia laughed.

Mr. Ray finally walked in. He was holding a pile of books. His very white bald spot was shining with sweat. "Sorry I'm late," he panted. "Can't seem to get all the books I need." He started handing out some novels. I picked one up and read the title *I Know Why the Caged Bird Sings*. "You'll be partnered up to share the books." There were some protests, but he paid no attention. "Maya Angelou is a powerful African-American author. She gives us a glimpse into what it was like to grow up black and female in the 1930s and 40s."

"Do we have to read this?" Eddie Franklin fussed. He

stood up and walked over to Rose. He put his arm around her. His arm rested against her naked neck. His skin was a shade darker than hers. "I know all there is to know about black women."

Rose shoved him away. "You wish!"

"That's enough, Mr. Franklin. Have a seat." Mr. Ray pointed a finger at Eddie. Eddie rolled his eyes and stepped away from Rose. He was tall with his hair in cornrows that needed to be redone. When he smiled you could see all of his white teeth. Girls who didn't know him would have said he was handsome at first sight. But we didn't. He always acted like a jerk. That made him ugly. He hadn't always been that way. Six years earlier he'd been nice enough. Then something happened. We all blamed it on puberty.

Rose gave Tia and me a look of disgust. "Creep!" She used to really like Eddie. But he was going about it all wrong. She was losing interest quickly.

"Ms. Cooper and Ms. Stone, you will be partners." Mr. Ray spoke without looking up from his class list. Tia and Rose smiled. It would be easy for them to share a book. As Mr. Ray kept calling out partners, I looked around the room. I knew everyone but didn't really feel close to anyone except Rose and Tia. But they were partners. That left me with someone I wasn't friends with.

"Ms. Powell." I looked up to hear who would be my partner. "You will share a book with Mr. Henry." I turned my head to find Mike Henry briefly glance at me and then glance away. He was okay looking but really shy. He stood a full head taller than me and was really skinny. His dark skin, though, was flawless. He always had his hair cut short. I never paid him much attention. I just hoped he didn't stink. I couldn't stand guys who stunk.

Rose leaned into me. "Don't worry. Nate won't get jealous."

I rolled my eyes, "Very funny."

Mike glanced at Rose and then quickly looked away. I shoved her. "See what you've done!"

"You'll be okay, Mikey, right?" Rose yelled across the room.

Mike looked up for a moment and then looked down again as he shook his head. He was trying to ignore Rose.

Once the books were all passed out, Mr. Ray started teaching. It was hard to listen. He said something about all of us learning from other people's stories. But I was too focused on mine.

I wasn't sure how long Nate's parents would put up with me. I could hear them arguing through the walls at night. They argued about me. I heard something about money and something about Nate graduating soon. He didn't need to be responsible for me. I would cover my head to block out the rest of what they said. In the morning his father wouldn't look at me, and his mother put on her best fake smile.

"Isn't that right, Ms. Powell?" Mr. Ray's voice broke into my thoughts.

"I'm sorry, Mr. Ray. Could you repeat the question?" I asked. I could feel a few giggles. I didn't pay them any attention.

Mr. Ray forced a smile. "Please pay attention, Ms. Powell." He cleared his throat. "Isn't it true that there are times we are all unhappy caged birds?"

I paused and looked at the board. What was he talking about? I had missed a whole lot. The board had the title written down. Beneath it were the words First Impressions of the Title. I took a breath. This was just my first impression. I hadn't missed much after all. "I, uh … I …" I had to think. After a moment I answered. "I guess it depends on what the cage looks like."

A few people giggled. Mr. Ray was calm. "Can you explain that, Ms. Powell?"

"Well," I paused again. "I guess some birds have huge cages and can walk or fly around in them. They never really want to get out. They have no problem thinking that the cage is their world. They don't even know they're in a cage. Then there are others who have really small cages. They can see through their bars and want what's on the other side." The room was silent. I felt stupid and added, "Or something like that."

Mr. Ray smiled. This time it was real. "Very good,

Ms. Powell. Very good." He looked at the rest of the class. "Please get with your partner and plan a reading schedule."

I was happy he changed the subject. I quickly grabbed the book and headed to the back of the room toward Mike. He pretended not to see me coming. I plopped down next to him. "Okay, let's get this over. You get it one week, and I get it the next."

There was a short pause, and then I heard his voice. It was soft, but strong. "That won't work."

"Excuse me?" I was trying to make eye contact. I was a little put out with having to work with Mike. I was not hiding it well.

"It won't work. We need to switch every day." He pretended to write something down.

"Okay. Whatever." I stood up. "I'll take it tonight." He just nodded, and I left to go back to my seat.

CHAPTER 6

Just a Look

When class was finally over, I found myself in the hall looking for Nate. He was leaning against a locker at the end of the hall. I smiled and started walking toward him. Just then the prettiest white girl in school walked up to Nate and said something. He laughed and followed her with his eyes as she turned to leave. Her perfectly straight long, black hair moved gently with her hips.

"What was that about?" I didn't hold back my flash of anger.

"What?" Nate looked at me like I was crazy.

"I saw you look at Bella!" I was looking down the hall to see if she was still around. I would give her a piece of my mind if she was.

"What? I can't talk to another girl?" Nate sucked air through his teeth. "Neema, don't you start going all crazy on me!"

I stood a moment and stared at the only boy I had given

my whole self to. I couldn't stand the thought of him even looking at anyone else. I dropped my eyes to stare at the tiles on the floor. I was trying not to cry.

"Come on, baby." Nate pulled me close. I took a deep breath. I was soothed by his sweet smell. "You know you're my girl."

I let him hold me a minute longer. I whispered, "I know."

As I lifted my eyes, I saw Eddie. He was walking past us and heading down the hall. For a moment he glanced at us. He quickly turned away. I saw him shake his head. It was a small shake, but it was there.

"What's his problem?"

"Who?" Nate asked. I didn't answer right away. "Neema, tell me who's bothering you, and I'll take care of him."

That was just it. He would yell at anyone I wanted him to. That was one thing I loved about him. But Eddie? Creepy Eddie? He wasn't worth a good yelling. "Nobody important really." I felt safe as long as Nate had his arms around me.

I spent the rest of the school day believing nothing would change.

CHAPTER 7

The Big Save

It felt good to be at work. As long as I kept my mind off of Mom, I would be okay. Saturdays were always spent at the Big Save. Crisis or not, I had to work. I needed some money to pay for the clothes I liked or the minutes on my phone. I had worked every Saturday since I turned sixteen. Sometimes they had me come in on Sundays. I was good at the register. Romero, my boss, said the customers liked my pretty face. I would tell Romero he was full of it. I liked the round Hispanic man. I thought he was probably fifty even though his constant smiling made him look younger.

"Sixty dollars and nine cents, please." I held out my hand as a small woman with red hair pulled out her wallet. She paid and left.

I felt Romero come up behind me. "You forgot to say thank you."

"Thank you." I yelled at the back of the woman as the sliding glass doors closed behind her.

Romero was still behind me. "Today's good work is tomorrow's job." It was his favorite saying.

I turned and faced my boss. "Are you saying I don't have a job next Saturday?"

Romero smiled at me. "Don't know yet." He started to walk away and turned his head to yell, "Just be nice to the customers."

"Yeah, Yeah!" I whispered. A large woman wearing too much yellow started unloading her pile of hot dogs and sugar cereal. I looked at her and gave her my best smile, "Did you find everything okay?"

She smiled back, "Why thank you. I sure did."

I looked at Romero who silently clapped for me.

The Big Save made me feel like nothing was going on in my world. Just food and money. Back and forth. Romero teasing. And at the end of the day I made a few dollars.

CHAPTER 8

Out

She's got to go!" Mr. Boyd's voice was loud, and he was standing in the kitchen. He wasn't even trying to hide how he felt. I sat on the couch that had become my bed. It had been two weeks since I moved in.

"Where's she supposed to go, Dad?" Nate was trying to talk sense into his father.

"I don't know! Has she even tried to find another place?" Mr. Boyd turned to me. He spoke to me for the first time since I moved in. "Have you even tried to find another place?" I couldn't answer. Not because I didn't know the answer. I was ashamed. I hadn't asked anyone else to take me in. Not even my own family. "Well?"

"No, sir," I finally answered.

He pulled out his cell phone and slung it on the couch. "Call someone now!"

I looked at the phone and picked it up. I stood to hand

it back to him, "Mr. Boyd, I can use my own phone. I don't want to use your minutes."

He grunted, "What? Now you're concerned about taking my money?" He grabbed his phone.

I felt a lump in my throat. What was he talking about? "I … I … I haven't taken your money."

"Dad!" Nate was yelling now. He came up next to me and put his arm around me. "Leave her alone."

But he didn't leave me alone. "Where do you think the food you've been eating comes from? What heats up the showers you've been taking?" I didn't answer. So he did. "My money! That's what. You haven't even offered to give me any of your money from work."

Tears started to flow. I couldn't help myself. I opened my quilt and started throwing my things on top of it.

"What are you doing?" Nate asked.

"Leaving," I sobbed.

"Dad, you can't just kick her to the street." Nate yelled. But Mr. Boyd turned his back and walked into his bedroom.

I could hardly see through my tears. I finally pulled the quilt ends together and tried to lift the pile. Nate grabbed it. "Let me help you." He slung the quilt bundle over his shoulder while I grabbed my purse and jacket.

We both walked down the stairs. Silence hung between us. When we got outside, the cool air hit me and made me catch my breath.

"Where are you going to go?" Nate shifted the quilt to his other shoulder.

"Aunt Amina," I answered so quickly that Nate frowned.

"You think she'll take you?" he asked.

"I know she will, and I don't even need to call." I couldn't look at Nate. "I used to stay with her off and on when I was younger. She's like a second mother to me."

Nate was quiet for a minute. He was thinking it through. I could tell he wasn't happy with me. "So all this time I thought you had nowhere to go?"

I finally looked him in the eye. He was still frowning. "No, Nate. I never said I had nowhere else to go."

"You made me believe that!" His voice was getting louder.

"I wanted to be with you." I stepped in closer and tried to touch his chest. But he stepped back.

"You lied!" Nate's face suddenly looked disgusted.

I panicked. "But Nate. I didn't lie! You know that! You were the first to take me in."

"You made me think I was your only hope," Nate snarled.

"I didn't make you." I was starting to cry again. Why was he reacting this way?

He shook his head. "Yeah, you didn't make me! I just fell right into the trap." He started to walk away from me. I followed him. His steps were fast, but I kept up.

"I would never trap you!" I grabbed his arm. "Please, Nate. Believe me. I love you!" By now I was crazy. I couldn't lose Nate. I couldn't.

He stopped. His look of disgust was gone. "Okay, Neema."

I searched his eyes. They were telling me nothing. "Okay what?" I asked as he began to walk again. We were close to his car.

"Okay. I believe you," he finally said.

I took a breath. I didn't know what to say. He said he believed me but something had changed. The panic I had felt was not as strong, but it was still there.

He piled my things into his car, and I jumped in the front seat. I told him where Aunt Amina lived. We drove the five blocks in silence.

A few flurries greeted me as I stood on the curb in front of Aunt Amina's apartment building. There was no grass, no trees, only concrete. I was standing right in front of the door. The building that towered above me blocked any late afternoon sun. I shivered from the cold.

"Can you get it from here?" Nate asked as he placed the quilt bundle at my feet. I didn't care that the quilt would get a little wet from the sidewalk.

"Yeah, I'm good," I lied.

Nate stood awkwardly in front of me. I wanted him to

reach out and hug me. Kiss me. He forced a smile. "I'll see you at school tomorrow."

"Okay … yeah." I felt like I was talking to a stranger. "See you tomorrow." He turned to get back in the car. "Nathan," I yelled with tears flowing. "Please!"

He looked at me. I had used his formal name. I must have been desperate. I must have looked like a mess. I knew my makeup was all smeared. He smiled. He walked back over to me. He took me in his arms and hugged me. "There's something hot about your bag-lady look."

I felt my body relax in his arms. "I love you!"

"I know." Nate kissed me and turned to go. I suddenly felt so tired. The day had been too much.

CHAPTER 9

Aunt Amina

Neema, get yourself in here." Aunt Amina stood taller than me and had Mom's same smooth, brown cheeks. Unlike Mom, Aunt Amina kept her hair in a simple short cut. She always said she didn't have time to fuss with looking good. But somehow she always looked good. She liked her earrings and was wearing a huge pair of gold hoops. "I wondered when you'd show up here."

I pulled my quilt bundle into the small living room. With a small couch and large brown overstuffed chair the space was simple and neat. I plopped the pile down on the soft, tan carpet. "What do you mean?"

"Well," Aunt Amina picked up my pile and walked me through the living room down a short hall into one of the two bedrooms. The bedrooms shared a bathroom between them. "I have your room made up for you. Your momma called after you left and was worried. She hoped you'd come straight to me. She even brought a few boxes full of your things."

"She called you? She came by?" I had pushed the thought of my mother away for two weeks. It was easier than thinking about what she'd done to me.

"Of course." Aunt Amina put her hands on her hips. "You don't really think she's that awful."

"She did kick me out!" I felt anger start to build.

Aunt Amina put her arms around me. "I know. She was wrong and still is wrong." She couldn't hide her own anger. "She needs to leave De Monte! What a good-for-nothing, low-down sleazebag!"

I suddenly laughed. It felt good to hear someone else talk trash about De Monte. Aunt Amina looked at me surprised, and she started laughing too.

I walked over to the neatly made bed. A small pink pillow stood out. It was a lopsided heart. I sat down and held the pillow in my arms. "I remember when I made this for you."

Aunt Amina sat down next to me. "I do too." She took a deep breath. "I need you to pretend this is your room."

Two large boxes stood in the corner ready for me to unpack. I looked at her and wasn't sure what she was trying to say. "I already feel that way."

She slapped my leg a little too hard. "Good! Then you need to treat this place and me like we are family." I was quiet waiting for her to finish. "That means no running around at night with boys."

"What?" I stood up and looked down at my aunt. "Do you think I run around at night? Do you think I'm a …" I couldn't say the word.

Aunt Amina stood up so she towered over me again. "Well, your mother …"

"She doesn't know anything! Remember, she kicked me out!" I was yelling now. "I have been out nights but only with Nate." I took a breath. "I've been with him the last few weeks. At least he took care of me."

Aunt Amina threw her hands into the air. "Okay, okay. I believe you." She said it, but I didn't think she meant it. "Just unpack your stuff and bring me that quilt. It needs a good washing." She left.

I stood alone in my aunt's guest room. Now my room. Why did it feel like I was being questioned? Why did it feel like nobody believed me? The stress was too much. I crashed on the bed and fell asleep.

CHAPTER 10

Curfew

Curfew?" I looked at Aunt Amina with disgust. "I'm almost seventeen and you're giving me a curfew?" I'd been at Aunt Amina's for a week. I had managed to take off evenings to be with Nate. Most nights I didn't get home until one in the morning. Aunt Amina was always waiting, sitting in her overstuffed chair. She'd look at me, shake her head, and go to bed. She was obviously not happy. I could hardly keep my eyes open at school, but I wasn't going to tell her that.

Aunt Amina kept cutting the pizza she'd pulled out of the oven. It smelled so good, but I was too mad to enjoy it. "If you're going to live with me, you have to go by my rules." She didn't raise her voice.

"I never had a curfew in my own house!" I was raising my voice. How could she do this to me?

She turned to look at me. Her eyes were strong and meant business. "Seven on school nights and ten on the weekends." I glared back. She turned away to cut the pizza again. "I know it's hard for you, but you're so tired in the mornings. Coming in at one in the morning after you've been riding around with Nate, or whoever, will not be okay as long as you are with me."

"Whoever?" I was screaming now. "How can you say that? I only am with Nate. I have never had anyone else!"

"Do you have birth control?" She stopped cutting and pulled out two plates.

"I'm not stupid!" I was starting to cry. I was so angry. "I thought you cared about me. You sound like you think I'm some slut."

She stopped and stared at me. "I do not think you're a slut." I could see anger start to rise. "Neema. You are so young and so wide open to get hurt. I'm only trying to keep you safe."

"But I'm with Nate. He keeps me safe."

Aunt Amina took a deep breath. "But for how long, Neema? He's just a having a good time. What will happen when he's ready to have a good time with someone else?"

"Not Nate! He loves me. You don't know him like I do," I screamed.

She turned back around and put two pieces of pizza on each plate. "I guess if he loves you then he'll let you get your rest. You need to do well in school. He'll wait for you. Isn't that what love is?"

She pushed the plate toward me. I didn't touch it. I

turned and ran to my room. How could she keep me from being with Nate? I thought I would move out. But where would I go? Nate's family wouldn't take me in. Rose or Tia might. But they each had a handful of brothers and sisters I would have to share a room with, not to mention a bathroom. Here I had my own room and a clean bathroom. I knew Aunt Amina was serious. I had to live by her rules if I wanted to stay.

My phone went off. I'd gotten a text from Nate. "Be there at 8."

I burst into tears. What could I tell him? How would he take it? I held the phone and replied. "Can't be out after 7. Can be out till 10 on Fri and Sat." I pushed send. I took a deep breath and waited for the return text.

He quickly wrote back. "Are u kidding? Are u a baby?" I felt tears fall. This wasn't the response I wanted.

I wrote back. "I hate it. But got to have a place to live. Please help me thru this. Can u get me Sat at 5?" The time it took him to write back felt like forever. I calmed myself thinking he was writing some long response.

I was starting to worry as the phone stayed silent. Then it finally came. One letter. "K." How come it took him so long to respond? Who else was he texting? Did he really have to think that long about getting me?

I stretched out on my clean quilt that I had spread across my bed and fell asleep with the phone in my hand. I woke up because my stomach hurt. I was so hungry. It was eleven, and I'd already slept four hours. I tried to push away my worry about not seeing Nate. I opened the fridge and found my plate with pizza still on it. I pulled it out and saw a small piece of paper on top. It read "I know you're mad, but I want you to know I love you, Aunt Amina." I threw the paper in the trash. I wasn't ready to forgive her yet.

CHAPTER 11

Saturday

You okay?" Romero came over to me as I gave an old man his change. I was happy to be back at work. It was the one place everything seemed normal.

I smiled at Romero. "I'm fine. Just have a date tonight."

He raised his eyebrows. "Is he good to you?"

I laughed, "Since when do you care about my boyfriend?"

"Always!" Romero said seriously. Then he smiled. "I'm watching out for you, my girl." Then he started to walk away. He turned around and smiled, "Neema, you look tired. Do you want to go home a little early?"

I took Romero up on his offer. I wanted the evening to be perfect. A little extra time could only help.

I looked my best. I felt excited to spend some time with Nate. Alone. We'd seen each other at school, but he always seemed in a hurry to get to class or meet up with someone else. He'd kissed me but only quick. Like I was his sister. I pushed the growing worry away. Tonight we would get it all straight.

He was late. He didn't show up until seven. I was tired, even after getting home an hour early from work. Suddenly I felt I had wasted a full hour's pay waiting. I was trying to play it calm when Nate pulled up. I didn't want to spend the whole time fighting. So I put on my sweet voice, "Where you been?"

"What? You think I have to tell you everything?" His face was looking at the road as I sat next to him in his car.

I swallowed hard. I wouldn't start fighting. "No, baby. Just thought you were getting me at five. No big deal. Only wanted time with you." I reached out and touched his leg. He let me. He didn't say anything, so I spoke again. "I like the new paint on the car." He'd been fixing up his ride. A bright yellow streak had been sprayed over the new deep blue body paint.

Nate smiled a little. "Yeah, it looks good. Soon I'll fix up the inside. Maybe some new seats."

I was happy he was smiling. I scooted over to him as close as I could. That was the best part about the station wagon. The one big seat let me sit close. I felt his body relax some. He turned on the radio and let the music blast.

We drove to Burger King and got some fries and a couple of burgers. Nate drove a few blocks further to an empty parking lot. We ate in silence listening to the beat of the songs, which seemed to tell our story. I finally spoke. "Look, Nate, I hate my aunt's curfew. It's killing me not to see you every night."

He finally looked at me. It was the first time that night he really looked at me. I thought his look was love. But maybe it was just pity. I couldn't quite tell. "I know. It sucks."

I smiled. "Yeah! It really sucks."

He shoved the last of his burger in his mouth. He was almost done chewing when he asked, "So what now?"

"What do you mean?" I felt my heart start to race.

"Well, if I can't see you but once or twice a week, do you still want this?" He said it like he was asking me if I wanted more fries.

"Say what?" I was trying to stay calm, so I shoved one french fry into my mouth. I wished I hadn't because I could hardly swallow it.

"Us." He took a sip from his drink, but I could hear he was just sucking air.

The look of panic flooded across my face. I couldn't hold my control anymore. "*Us* means everything to me. I love you." He didn't answer. Tears started to flow. "Are you breaking up with me?"

He still didn't answer. So I pulled in close to him. I started kissing his cheek. His neck. He didn't say anything but gave in to my touch. I don't know if it was the music blasting or if he really felt something for me. I thought his actions were letting me know he still loved me because he still made love to me. That's what I thought.

CHAPTER 12

Friend?

Wake up." Mike shoved me. I jumped up. Class was over.

"I fell asleep again?" I asked. I looked around and even Mr. Ray had left the room. So much for a teacher who paid attention. "Where's Rose? Tia?" I was suddenly upset. Had my friends even forgotten to wake me up?

"After two weeks of you sleeping in class, can you blame them?" Mike stood over me. He turned to leave but then stopped. He looked at me, and I saw his eyes drop for a moment. He looked almost shy. Then he looked at me. "Are you okay?"

I frowned. "Yeah. Of course. Why?"

He shook his head. "You're kidding, right?"

I kept frowning. "No."

He sighed. "Think about it, Neema. I've known you for ten years. I've never seen you sleep in class. Never!"

"Ten years?" I said out loud, wishing I hadn't.

He shook his head. "I guess you only see who you want to see." He turned to leave.

I jumped up and gathered my stuff together. I followed him out the door. "Wait!" He stopped. I saw his dark brown eyes for the first time. They looked hurt.

"What?"

"Why did you wake me?"

"Right now, I'm wondering that too!" He took a deep breath. I stared at him. "Are you going to just look at me or are we done?"

"Oh, sorry." I awkwardly shifted my books from one arm to the other. They touched my breasts, and I suddenly flinched. My breasts were so sore. I quickly recovered, not wanting Mike to think I was strange. I reached into the pile in my arms and pulled out the small book. "Here, it's your turn."

"Keep it. I think you need more time with it." He smiled a little. "I read ahead."

"Thanks." I smiled. He turned to go. "Mike?"

"Yes?" He halfway turned around.

"I mean thanks for waking me up."

He nodded and moved on. I watched him blend into the crowd that was gathering in the hall. I couldn't figure him out. But it only took two minutes for me to forget about Mike because I saw Nate duck into an open door and someone with long black hair following him.

CHAPTER 13

Fire

I don't know what happened. Something went off. It was like a fire blazed through my whole body. I couldn't see straight. I dropped all of my things on the floor. I didn't even see the people I shoved out of the way as I headed for the open door. The smell of perfume made my insides turn. I pushed away my need to puke.

I was breathing hard by the time I stood in front of the couple. The couple that was not me and Nate. The couple that was Bella and Nate. His gentle touch was on her hip, not mine. His dark skin was pressed up against her pale cheek as he kissed *her*. Not me.

I screamed as I flung myself at Bella and started hitting her. She screamed.

"Stop it, Neema!" Nate tried to pull me off.

Then I turned on him and started hitting him. "How dare you!" Tears made it hard to see his eyes. But I could smell his breath. It stunk for the first time. He smelled like her. By that time other students had stopped in the doorway to watch. They began to push into the room.

I couldn't take it. Nate had me pinned. "It's over," he yelled. "You crazy woman!"

I pushed him off of me. I didn't need to be able to see where I was going. The girl's bathroom was around the next corner. I ran into the first stall and puked. Tears and sobbing only made my heaving worse.

I didn't understand. How could the man I love drop me so easily? He loved me. Didn't he?

CHAPTER 14

Rose and Tia

Neema, are you okay?" Rose's voice seemed sweet on the other side of the bathroom stall door.

"No," I cried.

"Let us in." It was Tia. They had both found me. I figured it wasn't hard since the whole school probably knew what had just happened.

"Mike told us what happened," Rose explained. I guess he had followed the crowd.

I opened the door, and they both tried to squeeze in. It didn't quite work, so they left the door open. "You look awful." Rose was trying to pull me up. "Let's get you to the sink so we can clean you up."

They pulled me over and took some paper towels and wiped me off. I couldn't help but see myself in the mirror. My hair had fallen down around my face with small pieces of spit and vomit plastering it to my face. "I can't go back to class," I cried.

"Oh, yes you can!" Tia had her hand on her hip. "We're not going to let you run from that jerk."

They cleaned me up, and Rose took out some makeup. I let her make me look better.

"He broke up with me," I whispered.

"I guess him kissing Bella was a hint," Rose joked. I started to cry again.

"Smooth move!" Tia fussed.

Rose rolled her eyes. "Well, Nate may have one fine body, but I never trusted him!"

"What?" I looked at Rose in shock. "You never told me that."

Rose kept fixing my hair. "Really, Neema, I don't trust any man. They're all after one thing!"

"That's not true!" I couldn't believe I was defending Nate.

"Isn't it?" Rose looked at me with a listen-here-idiot look. "Think about it. Once he couldn't have you all the time, what happened?"

"Dumped you, that's what!" Tia answered for me.

I tried to pull myself together. There was some truth to their words. Had I been that blind? I took a deep breath. "I know you're telling me this to make me feel better, but it's not helping." I paused and then spoke without caring how stupid I sounded. "I love him."

"You may love him. But he don't love you." Rose was

almost finished with my makeup. "Now stop crying or I'll have to start over again." She turned me to face the mirror. "Anyway. You come on to this great party I'm having this weekend. I'll fix you up with someone else. It will get easier. The first time is the hardest."

First time? More times? More breakups? More hurting? I didn't like Rose's take on my breakup. I didn't want to cry again, so I didn't respond.

I tried to push my feelings away. I took a few deep breaths. I saw myself in the mirror, and I almost looked good. My eyes were a little puffy, but that was it. Tia leaned into me, so I could see her in the mirror too. She was smiling. "See how beautiful you are? You go out there and make him wish he'd never let you go."

In a sick way, that gave me strength. "You're right!" I tried to smile. "I'll show him what he's missing." Then maybe he'd want me back. I didn't share that last thought with my friends.

As we finally walked out the bathroom door, I couldn't help but feel I needed to puke again. I thought breaking up was making me sick. I let the wave of sickness pass and went to my next class hoping I wouldn't need to bolt for the door.

CHAPTER 15

Games

It wasn't easy pulling myself together. But I did. The next day I put on a white shirt that was cut low and tight. It was Nate's favorite. It seemed tighter across my bust than before, but that drew more attention to my shape. I wore my jeans that fit like a glove and high heels to make me walk with just the right amount of hip motion. I looked good. I walked past Nate and Bella in the hall and didn't turn my head. But other heads turned. A few guys came up to me and tried to talk to me. They couldn't keep their eyes off me. Even Eddie Franklin came up to me.

"Hi, Neema." He tried to slide his arm around my waist. "Looking good."

I shoved him away. "Don't touch me, creep."

Eddie kept up his smile and stayed close. "Come on. You cut me deep. I hear you're on your own again." He tried to whisper in my ear. "I'd love to hook up with you."

Suddenly I felt like I needed to puke again. I shoved

Eddie away from me a little too hard. "Shut up." I swallowed hard to control my stomach. "I thought you liked Rose. You really don't have a clue about girls, do you?"

Eddie's look changed for a minute. He seemed almost upset, but then he put on his fake smile again. "I'm still single. Doesn't hurt to try." Then he turned and left. I didn't get him. He always seemed creepy, but maybe he was just trying too hard.

"Remember the party tonight." Tia passed by me on her way to the restroom. I had forgotten that Tia was having a party, even though it was on a Tuesday night. I'd tell Aunt Amina I had to study at Tia's. I'd get around the curfew.

I waved at her and yelled, "I'll be there!" I looked at Eddie again thankful he was not invited.

Before I turned the corner to go into my English class, I had another guy flirt with me. I was quickly realizing my hot look and new status was giving me more attention than I could handle. If I was going to make Nate jealous, I would need to find someone who didn't creep me out.

"Hi, Mike," I said a little too sweetly as I sat down next to him. He looked at me and frowned. Then he opened *I Know Why the Caged Bird Sings*. I sighed, aware of how little I had been focusing on my school work. I was pulling a D in English, and that was because Mr. Ray was kind. He gave me a grade for my lame answers. I hadn't even participated in the discussion about Marguerite being raped as a child. I remember waking up thinking at least the jerk was murdered, but then I went back to sleep.

I leaned into him, "Why do you keep your nose in the book?" I tried to sound like I was teasing. I gave him my best smile.

"Why don't you?" He looked at me. He wasn't looking at my body. He wasn't looking at my lips. He was looking right into my eyes.

I took a deep breath. I would not let Mike throw me off. He wouldn't be easy, but he also wasn't like the other guys. If he wanted to talk about the book I would. "Actually I do. I do it at home." He raised his eyebrows and gave me a whatever look. I dropped my eyes a little and confessed, "Okay, so I've been sleeping some in class." He gave me the look again. "Okay, I've been sleeping a lot. But not today. I really want to do better." Mike just shook his head and turned toward the front of the classroom. Rose walked in to take her seat. Mike's eyes followed her for a minute, and then he looked at the teacher again.

I turned around as Mr. Ray put up a quote from the book on the board. Mr. Ray read, "I was liked, and what a difference it made. I was respected not as Mrs. Henderson's grandchild or Bailey's sister but for being Marguerite Johnson." He paused and looked around the room. He saw me sitting up straight playing the perfect student role. "Ah, Ms. Powell, you've decided to join us today." A few giggles through the classroom made me shoot a couple of girls some evil looks. I looked back at Mr. Ray who was still focused on me. "Can you share with the class why you think Marguerite feels this way?"

I smiled and took a deep breath. I couldn't really let it pass, and I was already looking stupid. "Don't we all want to be liked? Liked for who we are …" I kept looking at Mr. Ray. But I could feel Mike's eyes on me.

"True, but why does Marguerite say this?" Mr. Ray was looking at me.

I paused a moment before Mike butted in, "Because she hadn't felt smart or beautiful or even wanted. It was the first time she felt like someone would listen to her. After this she dives into books that would eventually become her life." Mike paused. "She was beginning to discover who she really was," he concluded.

I looked at him. As Mr. Ray asked another question, I whispered to Mike, "I was just about to say that."

"Sure you were." Mike smiled. He smiled for the first time. I was taken for one moment by the beauty in his smile. I couldn't stop looking at him. His smile quickly faded, and he whispered one more thing, "Neema, don't pull me into your games."

I dropped my eyes. I was suddenly aware that Mike was not going to play along. He knew what I was up to. I felt ashamed. I dared to look up at him. He was still looking at me. He knew who I was. Unlike Marguerite, I was not happy about this. For the first time I didn't like what I was. I lifted my eyes to find Mike still looking at me. I whispered, "Okay, no games." Mike nodded and then we turned to listen to Mr. Ray

CHAPTER 16

Tia's Party

I had to go to the party even though I didn't feel great. The vomiting hadn't stopped, but I'd started to manage it by eating saltine crackers at lunch. Rose and Tia thought I was fighting some stomach bug. I swallowed, hoping the feeling would go away.

Tia liked to have parties at her house. It was easy. Her mom worked evenings, and she sent her brothers and sisters to a back room. She lived in a small house on a street with twenty other small houses. At the end of the street apartment buildings looked down on this old community. It wouldn't be long before the neighborhood would be torn down and new high-rises would take over. But for now Tia's house was the party house.

Sometimes a party meant five people showed up. Other times twenty or more. The rule was that Tia had the place, and everyone else brought food and drinks. Sometimes it was soda and chips. Other times a half-empty bottle of vodka or a few bottles of beer would show up. Tia always got rid of the evidence.

Music blasted as I walked into her house. This was going to be one of her bigger parties. I pulled off my jacket and threw it over my shoulder before I walked in. It was cold, but I looked good with tight jeans and a low cut shirt. I wanted guys to notice me. I wanted to be there.

"Hey," Tia yelled as I ran up the steps into the stuffy room. She smiled a little too big. "Tommy wants to meet you." Tia pointed at a very good-looking white boy. I had only seen him in the halls at school, but he'd never shown me any interest. He looked a little out of place, but he smiled at me as I talked to Tia.

"What are you doing?" I pulled Tia's arm so our backs were facing Tommy. I expected to pick out my own guy.

"Getting you right back in the game." She turned me around and pushed me toward Tommy. But I turned back toward her as she started to walk into the small kitchen.

"Tia," I yelled, "I want to pick …" I started, but she disappeared. I quickly ran down the hall into the small bathroom. The sink and toilet needed cleaning. I used the toilet, wishing I didn't always feel like I had to pee. I avoided touching the small rusty circles on the sink as I washed my hands. I looked into the small mirror above the sink. I still looked good. I was still in the game. You can do this, Neema! I took a deep breath and walked back into the crowded room.

I felt a hand touching my arm. "Hi, Neema," Tommy was in close, so I could hear him above the blasting music.

I turned to face him. "Hi, Tommy." His wavy, brown hair fell into his face. I could almost taste his aftershave. My stomach turned. I couldn't seem to get rid of my need to puke. I swallowed hard. "I need a drink." Maybe that would help.

Tommy smiled and walked over to the kitchen and came out with two plastic cups. He handed me one. I brought it up to my lips, but the smell of alcohol was too much. I guessed this wasn't one of Tia's alcohol-free parties. I handed the cup back to Tommy, "I need some Pepsi." He awkwardly took the cup and returned with some soda. I sipped the dark liquid, letting it settle my stomach some. Tommy drank what I assumed was not Pepsi.

"Let's dance." Tommy pulled me by the hand. He wasn't asking. I put my cup down on the window sill and let Tommy pull me in close. He didn't hesitate to rest his hands on my hips.

I told myself that this was good. Another man into me. A good-looking guy into me. He had the firm build of a football player. This was good too. We'd only spoken a few words to each other, but he seemed nice enough. I had to swallow a few times as the urge to puke kept creeping back up.

A few times I looked at his eyes. A deep blue held my attention, and then we'd both laugh as if we'd told the

funniest joke. Then he kissed me on the neck. I told myself
it felt good. Another man. This was good. I needed another
man. What would I be if I didn't have a man? He kissed the
other side of my neck. I let him.

As one dance turned into two, I found myself still
being held by Tommy. Then it happened. He covered his
mouth over my lips. I would say it was a kiss, but it wasn't.
As soon as the taste of alcohol hit my lips I lost it. Vomit
spewed all over Tommy. He stood back with shock in his
eyes. Pepsi and some crackers I ate earlier were oozing
down his front. I thought for a moment he would vomit too,
but he cursed and ran from the room. Everyone had stopped
dancing and was staring at me. Disgusted. I couldn't believe
what had just happened. I was so embarrassed. So I ran too.
I ran outside and continued to puke in the street. My heart
was racing. How could I have let it get this far? Don't cry!
Don't cry! I swallowed hard and held it together.

Tia ran out after me. "Are you okay?"

"I'm better now." I stood up straight, looking over
Tia's shoulder into the house. I was wondering if Tommy
was okay. "I don't know what happened." I looked at Tia,
"I guess Tommy won't be asking me out anytime soon." I
must have looked like a total idiot to Tia.

"You think?" Tia started laughing. I tried to laugh, but it
wasn't funny. One day it would be funny. But at that moment
it wasn't. At that moment I knew I didn't have a stomach bug.

CHAPTER 17

Late

I sat naked on my bed. The mirror was directly across from me. My breasts looked bigger than usual, and I could hardly touch them because they were so sore. Fear slowly crept over me.

"It can't be," I whispered to myself. But even I couldn't deny the changes I was going through. My period was two weeks late. Not to mention me puking all over Tommy. I pushed the embarrassing moment away. How long had I been pregnant?

I slowly put on my most comfortable bra and wore a loose fitting top. My jeans still fit me nicely; in fact they were a little loose. I'd lost a few pounds from vomiting and not eating much.

I walked out into the living room with my jacket in my arms and faced Aunt Amina who was sitting on the over-stuffed chair eating a bowl of cereal. She looked up at me and frowned. "What's wrong?"

"I need to miss school today."

"Out of the question!" Aunt Amina stood up to feel my forehead. "Unless you have a fever, you're not missing school."

I spoke clearly and slowly. "I need you to take me to the health department."

Aunt Amina stopped touching my forehead. It only took a minute for her to put her hand up to her mouth. "Oh, no! You're pregnant?"

"I don't know for sure," I said, finally looking her in the eye. I had tears in my eyes. "I don't know how this could have happened. I've been taking the pills."

Aunt Amina went to the kitchen and put down her cereal bowl. She grabbed her keys and purse. "Let's go then. Let's not worry until we find out for sure. If you've been taking your pills, then I'm sure it's nothing. Just a little stressed out with everything that's been going on." She reached out her hand to me. Like a little girl, I took it. She guided me down the stairs. The fresh air felt good. Spring was around the corner. I hoped Aunt Amina was right. But I'd been telling myself those same lies for a few weeks now.

We took the subway for eight blocks. The smell seemed worse than ever. After we got out at Center Street, we walked along the wall leading us out of the underground. Suddenly the smell of piss was strong. I couldn't hold it anymore. A wave swept over me, and I puked all over the side of the subway-station wall. It didn't really make the wall look any worse. Or smell any worse.

Once I stopped puking and wiped my lips on my sleeve, I looked at Aunt Amina. Her hand was over her mouth again. Then she slowly pulled me into her arms. "Maybe it is what you think it is." I started to cry. She began to rock me. People walked past us like we were another pillar they had to pass on their way to work. "Don't worry. You're not alone." I felt great relief flood over my body. I didn't realize how alone I'd felt.

I couldn't speak. I just hugged her tighter. She didn't let go.

CHAPTER 18

Positive

I'd been to Central Street Clinic before. It was owned by the health department, and so I was able to get my birth control free. The building was clean and smelled like every other doctor's office I'd ever been in. We had to wait an hour before we were able to see the nurse. Aunt Amina sat in the front room and waited for me. She told me I could do this. She wouldn't leave without me. She smiled, and I tried to smile back. But I couldn't.

In a small room a young Hispanic woman took my blood pressure, weight, and a few other things I didn't quite understand. She didn't say anything nice to me. She didn't say much at all. I wondered if she thought I was a slut. Isn't that what everyone thought? She had me sit in a different small room. I waited for another ten minutes before a lady with blond hair that stuck up like a huge beehive came in and sat down across from me.

"Miss Powell?" Her white coat made her skin look

washed out. She was probably fifty and didn't know people didn't wear their hair like that anymore. But I really didn't care how she looked. She seemed kind.

"Yes, ma'am. Neema Powell." I spoke softly.

"I'm Nurse Jones." She shook my hand awkwardly. "So the paperwork says you think you're pregnant?"

"Yes, ma'am."

She opened a drawer and handed me a white stick. "I want you to go into the bathroom next door and pee on the stick and bring it back to me." She smiled. "Then we can take it from there."

I nodded and did as she asked. It didn't take long before I stood next to the nurse and handed the pregnancy test back to her. I could already see the double pink line forming. My heart raced. "Does that mean I'm pregnant?"

"It sure does. It's positive." She patted the chair next to her. "Have a seat, Miss Powell. Let's talk."

I felt myself sit down but was having a hard time listening. Pregnant? I felt trapped. How could I finish school? What boy would fall for me with a pregnant body or a baby on my hip?

"Miss Powell?" The nurse pulled me back. I finally heard her say, "You said your last period was around December fifteenth?" Nurse Jones was looking at the clipboard in front of her. She pulled out a small wheel and fiddled with it. "That would put your due date around …

September … twenty-first." She looked at me and smiled.

"But I can't be pregnant!" I was not ready to believe I could be having a baby. "I've been using birth control."

Nurse Jones put the clipboard down and asked, "Did you ever miss a day or two?"

I felt the heat rise. I had flashbacks to New Year's Day. "But only two days! I got right back on track."

The nurse tilted her head. She was trying to be as gentle as possible. "Didn't the nurse who gave you the pills explain if you missed a dose, even one, you should not have sex until you have your period and start the cycle over again?"

I frowned. I really couldn't remember. I was so eager to get the pills. I'd thought I was listening. "Maybe."

She reached out and patted my arm for a moment. "It will be all right."

"I don't know what to do." I started to cry.

Nurse Jones gave me a moment and handed me a tissue. "You're in your eighth week."

"How can that be? I had my period eight weeks ago." I blew my nose.

"That's right. We count how far along you are from the day of your last period. So the baby is about six weeks old, but you're in your eighth week of pregnancy."

"Whatever." I was too tired and upset to understand it all. "What now?"

The nurse became a little more serious. "You have choices you need to make."

I frowned. "What do you mean?"

She pulled out some papers with information about diet and what to expect while I'm pregnant. Then she looked at me. "You can decide if you are going to keep the baby or not."

My head started to spin. I felt like vomiting again. "You mean like abortion?"

"That or placing the baby for adoption." The nurse took a deep breath. "It's my job to let you know you do have choices to make. No one can make them for you."

I bolted from the room to the bathroom and vomited again. When I returned to the room, I found the nurse had not moved.

"I hate this vomiting." I was feeling a little better.

"It will usually pass when you are around your four-teenth week. But it's never the same for any two mothers." She had used the word mothers.

"I can't be a mother yet," I said out loud, wishing I hadn't.

"Then you need to think about your choices." Her voice was serious again. "You also need to think about the role the father of the baby should play."

Nate. I knew it was Nate's baby. What would he say? I looked at the nurse. "Does he have rights?"

Nurse Jones lifted her eyebrows. "If you want him to." I must have looked confused, so she continued. "You have the right to choose how involved he is. If you can prove he is the father then he will be legally responsible to support the baby. But some families choose to leave the father completely out of the picture."

I felt my heart race. I wanted Nate in the picture. I couldn't get used to the thought of him not being in my picture right now. How could I even think about his role with our baby? "There's too much to think about." She could tell I was trying hard to hold it together.

Nurse Jones smiled. "Miss Powell, you are not alone." I looked at her confused again. "We'll help set you up with a doctor that takes Medicaid. It's up to you to keep your appointments." She paused for a moment. "If you choose to continue with the pregnancy."

I had so many questions racing through my head. How will I take care of the baby? How will I pay for it? How can I finish high school? But I just couldn't ask them. Not yet. I had to first decide if I would be a mother or not.

I thanked the nurse and took all the paperwork with me. I handed Aunt Amina the papers and the note for my first doctor's appointment. The look in her eyes was not one of pity. She was not upset. She looked in control. She knew strength. She knew survival. I was thankful she was on my side.

CHAPTER 19

Choices

I didn't even try to look good at school the next day. I pulled my hair back in a tight ponytail and threw on my loosest top. I couldn't stand the thought of anyone hitting on my pregnant body.

"What happened to you?" Rose walked by me as we were getting ready for Mr. Ray to come in.

I thought I would tell my girlfriends everything. But I wasn't ready yet.

"Just a stomach bug," I lied. "Feel better today though."

"Don't look it." Rose sat down and Mike walked up to his seat next to me. Rose looked at Mike. "You look good though! See if you can rub some of that off on Neema."

Mike turned and smiled at Rose. "Was that a compliment from Queen Rose?"

Rose put her hand on her hip. "Oooh, Mr. Mike has a voice."

Mike looked away from Rose and stared at me. He frowned slightly. Then he smiled. "No games today?"

I couldn't smile back. I was ticked that he was making a joke out of how I looked. Then I realized he was trying to cheer me up. I shook my head. "No games."

"Good." He handed me the book. "Your turn to read the ending tonight." I felt his hand touch mine as I took it from him. He didn't pull away. I was confused. He wasn't hitting on me. He was just touching me. He wanted me to listen to him. So I looked at him as he said, "I think you'll really like it." Then he let go. His look and smile were gone. He was all focused on Mr. Ray and the next question.

I couldn't listen. I couldn't stop thinking about the choice I needed to make.

That night Aunt Amina didn't say anything as I went to my room early. I jumped in bed at seven and pulled my quilt over my body. I pulled *I Know Why the Caged Bird Sings* out of my huge purse lying next to me on the floor. The papers Nurse Jones had given me fell out of the bag.

I picked up the paper that told about the week by week development of the fetus. I found eight weeks. A small peanut-looking form with eyes and small arms and legs stared at me. I couldn't believe the baby was already a little human. I quickly shoved the papers under my bed. I'd look at them later. I had to finish the book.

I became lost in the pages of this book for the first time.

I was sorry I hadn't given it my full attention before. In the last chapters Marguerite, who is now called Maya, goes through a change. She feels stronger about knowing who she is. And when she is faced with a surprise pregnancy she doesn't know what to do. But she finds strength. She finds her baby son touching her. He knows she is his mother. He gives her all the trust in the world. Maya's mother says, "See, you don't have to think about doing the right thing. If you're for the right thing, then you do it without thinking."

As I put down the book, I cried. I didn't know what I was crying for. What was the right thing? I touched the cover of the book. I wasn't the only one who had been young and pregnant. But that didn't make it any easier. I still had to make a choice.

I put my head on the pillow and let my hand fall to the floor. I pulled the paper out from under the bed. I touched the small peanut. I knew what I would do. I had known from the minute I sat naked in front of the mirror. I knew I would choose to be a mother. I just didn't know if I was strong enough.

As I drifted off to sleep, I had a strange thought. Why did Mike tell me I would like this part of the book? I let the thought fade as I gave in to sleep.

CHAPTER 20

Nothing New

Aunt Amina was sitting in her overstuffed chair with her bowl of cereal. I sat down across from her on the couch. "I'm keeping the baby." I was a little more forceful than I had planned to be. Guess I didn't want her to think I was asking a question.

Aunt Amina sat up straight. She slowly put the bowl down on a small table next to her. She looked at me with serious eyes. "Of course you are." She frowned a little. "Were you thinking of an open adoption?" Her eyes got wide. "Or abortion?"

I suddenly felt a little stupid. "Well, the nurse said I needed to think about all my options." I dropped my eyes. "I guess I should have told you."

Aunt Amina got up to come sit next to me. She gently put her arm around me. "Sweet girl. Have you been worrying about the choices?" I nodded and felt like a five-year-old. "Well, the nurse had to tell you your options. In some cases you have to make other choices. But not in the Powell family."

I looked up at my aunt a little confused. "What's that supposed to mean?"

Aunt Amina sighed. "Didn't your momma tell you anything?"

"Tell me what?" I shifted my body to face my aunt a little better.

"That she had you when she was sixteen?" Aunt Amina said it like it was no big deal.

"She told me some." I didn't want her to think I knew nothing. I hadn't really thought about it much. Mom and I never really talked about her early life. I knew she had been a young mother, but I never did the exact math. She talked about my father as if he was an army man she fell in love with. But he left for the army before she could marry him. She said she never told him about me. When I asked why, she had told me he came back with another woman on his arm. It didn't seem the right time to break the news. "I always thought Mom was twenty and working."

"That's what your mom wanted you to believe. She didn't want the same thing to happen to you." Aunt Amina sighed again.

"I guess her plan didn't work," I laughed.

"Guess not." Aunt Amina smiled. "Wonder how she'll react."

My eyes got big. "You haven't told her yet?"

Aunt Amina shook her head. "Not my job. You have to tell her."

"I think she'll kill me." I leaned back against the couch.

"Yes, she will." Aunt Amina smiled. "But she'll do it with love." When I didn't laugh, Aunt Amina patted my leg. "Listen, Neema, your mom will know better than anyone else what you're going through. You might be surprised."

I stood to leave for school. Before I opened the door, I looked back at Aunt Amina. "Where were you when all this happened?"

She smiled. "I was with her all the way." She paused. "I won't raise your baby, Neema. But I'll be here for you. We Powell women stick together." I smiled. I knew Aunt Amina was telling the truth. But I couldn't picture my mother wanting to have anything to do with me or her first grandchild.

CHAPTER 21

Knowing

How did you know?" I walked up beside Mike as he was heading for English class.

"Know what?" Mike looked at me with a blank stare.

"That I would like the last part of the book," I stated. I moved in front of him. He had to stop. He towered over me.

He said it slowly like I was stupid, "Because it's good." He was looking around like he couldn't be bothered.

"I thought you said no games," I said to him.

Mike stopped looking around. He stared me straight in the eye. "Because you have all the symptoms." His eyes softened. "I pay attention." He tried to smile. He came in close and whispered in my ear, "Don't worry, I won't say anything. That's up to you."

I wasn't sure how to respond. I'd never met anyone like Mike. "Okay, good," I said awkwardly. But I wasn't done with him. I walked behind him into class, and we took our seats. "I don't get you."

He looked right at me. "You mean you've never had a guy as a friend?" I stared a minute. Then I suddenly got it. This was what it felt like to not be hit on. This is what it felt like to just talk with a guy. This felt good.

I smiled. "Yeah. I guess that's it."

He leaned in. "So you like the ending?" He was back to discussing the book.

"I said I did." I didn't move away. His closeness felt natural now. "I think Maya gives young women strength."

"To go through with it?" he asked. I knew very well we were not talking about the book anymore.

"To go through with it and keep the baby." I smiled.

"Maya wasn't going to give the baby away." Rose came up behind us and butted in. "I don't know what book you two read!" she teased.

Mike and I jumped. He looked at me, and I shook my head. He suddenly realized I hadn't told my best friends yet. He smiled at Rose. "You're right, as always."

She smiled back and flipped her hair. "You better believe it."

As she sat down, Mike looked at me again. I whispered, "Thank you."

He nodded and turned to look at Mr. Ray.

I didn't really know why I hadn't told Rose and Tia. They were my best friends after all. I told myself it had only been two days since I knew for sure. That wasn't long at all.

I had to work Saturday but not Sunday. We were planning to hang together. That would be the perfect time.

CHAPTER 22

Secret

I've got something to tell you." I was walking between Tia and Rose as we headed to the subway station. We'd decided to go see a movie together. The subway wasn't the perfect place to share my secret, but it would have to do.

"What is it?" Tia said as we headed down the steps into the station.

"I'm pregnant." I tried to sound like it was no big deal.

"What?" Rose stopped me at the bottom of the stairs. Her hand was on my arm. Tia moved in close. We were all huddled together.

"I'm pregnant." I smiled a little. There was something about sharing this big news with my best friends that made me feel almost happy.

Rose laughed out loud. Tia pulled me in close. "Is it Nate's?"

Rose hit her gently. "Stupid question! Of course *it's* Nate's." She paused and then eyed me. "Right?"

I pretended to be mad. "How dare you! Of course it is." I couldn't hide my smile.

"Does he know?" Tia asked.

My smile quickly went away. What role would Nate play? That question hadn't been answered yet. It hurt to think about it. I shook my head. "Not yet. And don't you dare tell him."

Rose put her arm through my arm as we continued to get in line for the subway. "Of course we won't tell. How far along are you anyways?"

"Eight weeks," I said.

"*Eight weeks?*" Rose made people look at us, so she quickly lowered her voice. "We're the first ones you've told, right?"

"Aunt Amina knows and …" Then I stopped. I wished I hadn't said and.

"And who?" Tia asked.

I rolled my eyes. "Mike."

"*Mike?*" Rose yelled again.

"Shh!" I hushed her. "I didn't tell him. He figured it out."

We stopped talking for a minute as the subway cars came to a screaming stop. As we took our seats and waited for the cars to get moving again, Rose said, "I guess that doesn't count."

I didn't know why it mattered really, but it was

bothering her. I added, "I haven't even told my mom yet."

That seemed to make it all better. Rose perked up. "Ooooh, she'll kill you," she teased.

"Yes, she will." I smiled at Rose and Tia. They were each linked into my arms, one on each side.

"I think it will be fun to have a baby around," Tia said. "It will be so sweet having a little baby that is all yours."

I hadn't thought about that at all. Right now I wasn't having too much fun puking and watching my body change before my eyes. But maybe it would get better.

CHAPTER 23

Mom

I wasn't happy with Aunt Amina when I got home from the movies. I had had a great day. Then I walked in, and there was Mom. She and Aunt Amina were sitting at the kitchen table with bottles of beer in their hands.

"Hi, Neema." My aunt was smiling. "Look who's here."

Mom and I stared at each other. I hadn't seen her for about eight weeks. Now she was coming by for a beer. I knew exactly what Aunt Amina was trying to do. But I knew it was all my aunt's doing. Not my mother's.

"Hi, Neema." Mom stood. Her hair hung awkwardly on one side, and her T-shirt was wrinkled. She looked like a dog that had been beaten. I didn't trust De Monte. He'd turned my strong mother into a fearful child.

I looked at her. I looked at Aunt Amina. I looked back at my mother, and I couldn't help myself. I spoke the first words to my mother in eight weeks. "I'm pregnant." Then I turned and walked to my room. It wasn't until I closed the door that I heard Mom's voice. She was yelling something and Aunt Amina was yelling back. I fell face down on my bed and covered my head with my quilt. I let the screaming turn into background noise. I cried.

Finally there was silence. I shoved the quilt off of me and sat up. I walked over to the mirror and stared at the pictures I had finally stuck along the mirror's edges. I touched the picture of my mother and me laughing and then pulled down the picture of my father.

"I'm sorry, Neema." I turned around to find my mother standing in my room.

"Don't you knock?" I turned back to face the mirror. She moved in closer. I could see her behind me in the mirror.

"I was young." She spoke softly. "I never talked about it because I didn't want you to think it was okay to get pregnant early." I didn't answer. I shook my head as I replaced the picture on the mirror. "He was a good man, your father." She paused. "But I really didn't know him very well. I lived in a small town about four hours south of here. I fell for your father when he was on leave from the army. He thought I was twenty and well, you know." I turned to look at my mother as she finally told me the truth. "He left, and I was pregnant with you. My parents thought it was a bad idea to tell him. I was only sixteen, and it would make things very hard."

"What do you mean?" I asked.

"He was twenty-five and it would not have been good for his family." She paused and added, "Or mine." She walked over to my bed and sat down. She suddenly looked very old.

"You're kidding!" It seemed so out of date. "Your parents cared how it looked to other people?"

Mom lifted her eyes to meet mine. "Times have changed so much, so fast." She shook her head. "That's when I left home and took off to the city. I hoped that I could make it on my own. Me and my baby girl." She shook her head. "Thank God for your aunt. She followed me and didn't let me do this on my own. She worked and supported all three of us until I finally found out I could do hair well. That's when I started at the beauty shop."

"And your parents?" I asked. I knew they had died in a car crash, but I was beginning to wonder if that was a lie too.

She halfway smiled and said, "They were happy that my sister was with me. They sent whatever money they could. Until they died."

"Why didn't you tell me this?" I was crying again. "I don't think any of that had anything to do with me getting pregnant, Mom." I was raising my voice now. "I missed taking two pills. Two stupid pills. That's what happened. It's not like I planned this or wanted it. It just happened." I was shaking now.

Suddenly I felt my mother's arms around me. "I know, baby, I know." I didn't pull back. I needed my mother. Even with the bad choices she'd made. She pulled my chin up, so I could look into her eyes. "I swear to you I will do everything I can to help you. We Powells stick together."

I smiled at the phrase my aunt had used earlier. Then I dropped my eyes. "I'm not moving back in with De Monte."

Mom smiled. "I hope not. He's a real creep. I'm moving in here."

"What?" My eyes were wide.

"That's why I came over. I was asking Amina if I could move in. I'm leaving De Monte."

"You mean Aunt Amina didn't call you and tell you to come over?" I felt guilty.

"No, I dropped in," Mom said.

"Oh," was all I could say. I had judged Aunt Amina. She hadn't set me up. Mom had finally left De Monte. I smiled at Mom. "Welcome home."

CHAPTER 24

Roommates

It took some getting used to. My mom shared my room. We bought a cheap foam pad and made a second bed on the floor next to mine. That lasted one night. I had to pee a couple of times, and Mom didn't like me stepping on her. So we moved her bed closer to the dresser. That worked. But when I got dressed in the morning, I was stepping over her to get to my things. Mom finally convinced Aunt Amina to let her sleep on the couch. She left her stuff in my room, but the couch allowed her to sleep a little better.

For the first time in a long time, I felt like I was part of a family. Mom started looking stronger. She focused on her customers again. She'd come home after eight o'clock but had a smile on her face as she talked about a new hair style that she couldn't wait to try out on me.

Aunt Amina would be gone during the day. She worked at the library. She had been there since she moved to the city. She didn't make great money, but the job was steady and she loved the quiet. She and I would take turns making dinner. We'd save a plate and join Mom when she'd get in from work.

The best part was that when I was twelve weeks pregnant, Mom and Amina came with me to my first doctor's appointment. They were there with me as Dr. Baker checked me. He was a little white man with no hair. He was gentle, and his smile was real.

"See that little peanut." Dr. Baker pointed to a small screen. It showed my first ultrasound. I could see the small fetus move around. A loud noise kept pounding away. I thought there was something wrong with the machine.

"Oh, Neema!" Aunt Amina took my hand and squeezed it.

Mom came in close to the monitor. "Is it just one?"

I suddenly panicked. "It better be!"

The doctor patted my leg. "There is only one fetus, and it looks very strong. Listen to that heartbeat!"

I frowned for a moment not knowing what he was talking about. Then I realized that the pounding was the sound of my baby's heartbeat. It was the sound that finally hit me. Not the small peanut on the screen. It just seemed like another picture. But the sound. My baby's heart. I was suddenly overwhelmed. It was real. It was really happening. A real life was forming inside me. I started crying.

"I know! It's wonderful!" My aunt smiled.

But I wasn't thinking that at all. I was scared. I had

never been that scared in my life. I turned to my mother. She bent down and kissed the top of my head and whispered, "Not alone." She knew. She had been here before.

I let my mother hold my hand as Dr. Baker spoke about what I should eat and how often I should come to the office. He finally handed Aunt Amina some papers suggesting classes for me to take. It was all a blur. I suddenly felt sick. Thank God the trash can was only a few feet away.

CHAPTER 25

Time to Tell

The nurse was right. I stopped feeling so sick when I hit the middle of my fourteenth week. My pants were too tight, so I stuck to wearing my cute dresses. My breasts were still changing, and I finally broke down and bought a bigger bra.

I looked in the mirror before I headed to school. My red dress came up a little above my knees. Even though I had a small belly on me, it wasn't too noticeable. Not yet. But it would be soon. I had to tell Nate. I didn't want him to hear it from anyone else. The thought made my chest hurt. I hadn't spoken to him since we broke up.

It was already March, and Nate would be graduating soon. I had to tell him while he was still in my life, even if it was only as another student in my school.

As I walked down the hall, I smoothed out my red dress. I at least knew I looked good. More importantly I felt good. I wouldn't run away from him this time and puke in the toilet. I would be strong. I had to be strong.

Nate had his back to me as he was getting some books out of his locker. Bella wasn't around. That gave me a little hope.

As I got close, I smelled him. The familiar odor made my insides turn. I pushed the flood of memories away. "Nate?" He turned around at the sound of my voice. He was holding his books and had a what-do-you-want look on his face.

"What?" He spoke as if I was bothering him. He looked around as if he was looking for Bella to show up at any minute.

I wanted to turn away and not tell him. I felt like he didn't deserve to know. But I suddenly touched my belly. If I didn't tell him now, rumors would spread, and he'd never believe me.

"Nate!" I said again with a little more force until he looked me in the eye. "We need to talk."

He frowned. "We got nothing to talk about. It's over. Can't you get that into your head?"

I closed my eyes for a minute. I could still picture my mother and Aunt Amina sitting on the couch that morning. They were like my small cheering team. Aunt Amina's words came to me, "Neema, remember. You tell him the truth. What he does with it is his business." I opened my eyes, and he was turning his back to me.

"Nate! Listen to me!" I grabbed his arm to get his

attention. He pulled away a little, but I tightened my grip. He frowned as I pulled in close. "I'm going to say this once. You can do what you want with it." I took a deep breath. "I'm pregnant."

He looked confused at first. Then his eyes grew wide, and he looked down at my stomach. "Whose is it?"

I rolled my eyes. "Yours, of course. Never has been anybody but you."

He pulled his arm out of my grip. "You're tricking me, Neema. You just can't let me go."

I shook my head. What he does with it is his business. I stepped in close to him again. "It hurt when you left me, Nate. And it's taken me two months to get over you. It took my friends and family to help me see the jerk you really are. But you will always be the father of my baby. What you do with that is your business."

"What's going on?" Bella came up behind us and put her arm around Nate.

Nate's eyes flew open. "Hey, baby." He was a little too sweet. "Nothing's going on. Neema was just moving on."

I could have been mean. I could have really made Bella mad. But I didn't. She'd find out soon. As soon as I stopped trying to hide my belly. It would be real.

I put on my best fake smile. "Hi, Bella. I am *definitely* moving on." One last look at Nate told him that I was telling the truth.

CHAPTER 26

Showing

Telling Nate about the baby made me feel so much better. I could focus on my school work, and I started wearing cute clothes to show off my growing belly as the weeks turned into months.

As my belly grew, a few students and teachers gave me mean looks. I felt the word slut thrown at me a couple of times, but for the most part, people left me alone. I tried to ignore the stares. Some days were easier than others. Even Tommy, who had ignored me since I threw up on him, took a minute to give me a dirty look. He just shook his head and turned away. I could see him mouth to his friend "What a waste!" People could be so hateful. So I stuck to my friends. They thought I was cute.

"Who you dressing up for?" Mike slid in next to me at lunch. Rose and Tia were sitting across from me. He'd been eating with us more often than not. We'd laugh and talk in class. Most days, school almost felt fun again.

"You, I guess," I teased. It was easy being with Mike. He was the first to know my secret, and now as others began to figure out I was pregnant, he felt somehow a part of my life.

He laughed. "You really are showing now." He pointed at the round, hard belly that was sticking out.

Right then I felt a small movement. It was a little ripple. I was almost five months pregnant, and I had been feeling some strange movement for a few weeks now. I grabbed Mike's hand and placed it on my belly. "Feel this!" Rose and Tia tried to reach over but gave up when they couldn't quite touch me.

Mike, though, held his hand there a moment. He was concentrating. "I don't feel anything."

Then I was aware of the warmth coming from his hand. He started shifting his hand around my belly. I quickly pushed his hand away. He frowned at me, "What's that about?"

I dropped my eyes. "I'm sorry. It's … it's …" I couldn't find the words. "It's been a while since a guy touched me."

Mike shook his head with a half smile. "Do you think every guy wants to get in bed with you?"

I frowned. "Don't you?"

He lifted his eyebrows. "Are you offering?" he teased.

"Very funny," Rose jumped in. She sounded almost jealous.

I hit Mike in the arm. "Stop messing with me!" I sighed. "You're not like any guy I've ever known."

"That's for sure!" Rose added.

"I take that as a compliment." Mike smiled at Rose and took a bite of his sandwich.

"You should!" I smiled at my friend. That's what he was. My friend. I had found myself half wishing he were more, but I knew that I needed his friendship. Nothing else. Rose, on the other hand, seemed to keep looking at Mike. Mike, though, seemed to be ignoring her.

"Hey." I looked up from my lunch and saw Eddie Franklin standing across from me. He was behind Rose and Tia. I hadn't talked to him since he came on to me in the hallway. He was holding a chocolate milk in one hand, and he was awkwardly waving at me with the other.

"Hey, Eddie." I gave a little wave to match his. Then I turned to talk to Mike again.

"I'm sorry." I heard Eddie's voice almost squeak. Both Mike and I looked at Eddie who took a swig of his chocolate milk. He suddenly spoke again, as if the milk had given him strength. "Look, Neema. I'm sorry. Okay?" It was like it didn't matter that Mike, Rose, and Tia were there. "I don't hit on pregnant women."

"Only everything else that has breasts!" Rose teased. Mike was trying not to laugh, but Tia was not holding back.

Eddie acted like he hadn't heard Rose or didn't really care what she said.

Eddie was waiting for me to say something. I was trying not to laugh, so I quickly said, "Thanks, Eddie. Good talking to you. See you around."

Eddie waited for a minute longer. "Okay, then. See you around." He started to walk away but turned again and added, "Hope you're doing okay. I mean with the baby and all. You'll have your hands full soon." I stared not knowing how to respond to this strange Eddie, as he finished. "So, um, see you around."

As he left, I looked at Mike and my girlfriends. "What was that all about?"

Mike shook his head. "I have no idea." We watched Eddie walk over to a group of girls who quickly moved out of his way.

We started laughing. But as I took one more glance at Eddie, I saw him look at me. I felt ashamed. I brushed the feeling away. Why should I care what Eddie Franklin thinks? He was too weird for me to care.

CHAPTER 27

girl

I couldn't believe it was already May. Nate would graduate soon. I was ticked that I couldn't completely push him out of my head. But sitting in the doctor's office waiting to find out the baby's gender made me think about him. It was his baby too! I pushed Nate out of my head as the nurse called my name.

"It's a girl." Doctor Baker pointed to the image of the fetus. He explained how he could tell. I simply nodded and took his word for it. A girl.

Mom and Aunt Amina each squeezed one of my hands. There would be four Powell women in our small apartment soon.

A girl. Would she be like me? Would she be like my mother or Aunt Amina? I suddenly hoped she'd be like none of us. I wanted her to be better. Make better choices. That was up to me. But how?

I looked at the little girl's image. My little girl. I would have to find a way.

CHAPTER 28

Nate's Graduation

I couldn't help myself. I went. I should have stayed home. But I went. I guess I thought one last look at Nate before he graduated would change something.

I stood in the back of the high school gym. Rows of metal chairs changed the feel of place. But the smell reminded all of us it was still a gym. The heat caused my yellow dress to stick to my body. I shifted from one foot to the other as my feet ached.

I caught a glance of Mr. and Mrs. Boyd sitting close to the front. They were proud to see their son graduate. They should be. Nate's little brothers stood fidgeting. I could tell they could care less about Nate's big moment. I smiled. They were, after all, my baby's uncles. I pushed the thought away. I couldn't think this way.

"What are you doing here?" Bella stood next to me. Her beautiful black hair was pulled up off her neck. Small wisps of hair fell gently to her shoulders. Her look, though, was not gentle.

"It's my school too!" I spat. "I can come to graduation if I want to. I have friends." I looked straight ahead.

"Yeah, right!" Bella crossed her arms.

I pointed to the stage. "You better not miss your boyfriend crossing the stage."

Bella turned red and looked at Nate. She almost missed his big moment because of an old girlfriend. I had to keep myself from laughing.

Bella left me and headed down the aisle to sit with the Boyds. I felt anger flood through me. How could they accept her and not me?

I watched the whole ceremony. Alone. My real friends had better things to do.

As it ended, I walked outside and welcomed the small breeze. It was warm, but it still felt good. I turned to head toward the subway. There were so many people. I tried to slip in and out between all the bodies. Suddenly I was face to face with the Boyds. They were smiling, but as they saw me the smiles faded. Both of Nate's parents dropped their eyes to look at my belly. They did not hide their look of disgust. They thought I was a slut. They always had. Just then Nate came up next to his mother and his smile faded fast. The four of us stood awkwardly.

"Hi," I said weakly.

The youngest brother came running up to me. "Hey, Neema. You going to have a baby?"

It was at that moment I knew. Nate hadn't told his parents. I glanced at Nate in shock. His parents exchanged looks. Their eyes grew big. But no one said anything.

I took a deep breath. "Yes, I'm having a baby." I looked at Nate one last time and whispered, "A baby girl." He dropped his eyes. He wasn't going to tell his parents. And they obviously wanted to pretend that it wasn't true.

So I turned and left. I pushed away my desire to scream. I pushed away the look in Nate's parents' eyes. I told myself I was better off having nothing to do with the Boyds. They were the ones choosing to deny their grandchild. I pushed away my anger at myself. How could I have been so stupid to think they would really care? If Nate didn't care why would they?

CHAPTER 29

Summer

Hot! Summer was so hot. The window unit didn't push out cold air fast enough. I tried to keep cool, but the only way it felt good was to sit in my bra and underpants in front of a fan. My belly was feeling more and more like a small basketball tucked under my skin. My belly button was almost gone and replaced by a wide, smooth dark spot.

Tia and Rose kept talking about how they couldn't wait for the baby to come. How they would make great aunties. Sometimes Mike would follow us as we all marched into Walmart and started picking out baby clothes. Mike would roll his eyes, telling us that we should save the money for important things like diapers. Then, the same evening, they would take me to a friend's house where a party was in full force. I felt like I was their pet. I enjoyed it.

During most days, I worked. I was happy that Romero took me on full-time at the Big Save during the summer. At least it was cool in the store. But my feet hurt like crazy.

Every time I asked to go to the bathroom, I felt like I was testing Romero's saying: Today's good work is tomorrow's job. I would ask to pee every half hour. But Romero would just smile, pat my belly, and shoo me off to the break room. He was good to me.

"Get down, Suzy!" I heard a voice I thought I recognized. I had left the restroom and turned into the cereal aisle. The voice was firm. "Suzy. Get down or you'll knock all the cereal down."

"But, Eddie, I want the Froot Loops." The small girl had her hands on her hips as Eddie Franklin stepped over to her. He had a baby boy on his hip and two little boys sitting in the shopping cart. The two boys had a box of cereal open and were eating one piece at a time.

"Okay, Suzy." Eddie's voice had softened. "Let me reach it." He handed the box to the little girl and then kissed the top of her head. Was this the same Eddie I knew?

"Eddie?" I asked, making sure it was him.

He turned to face me. His face dropped. The baby had spit up on his black T-shirt, and the white mixture had dried into a nasty crust. He shifted the baby into his other arm to try and hide the spot. "Uh ... Hi, Neema."

"Summer job?" I pointed at the cart full of kids.

"No." He tried to smile. "Well, sort of." He brushed the top of the heads of the two boys. "These are my brothers,

Leny and Dion. They're four and two." He reached out to the little girl who took his hand. "This is Suzy."

"I'm six!" She held out her fingers, trying to hold the cereal box at the same time.

Eddie nodded to the baby at his hip. "This is Gabe. He'll be one next month."

"Lots of small kids," I said smiling at the little baby who was trying to eat his whole hand.

"Yeah, my mother had me when she was young. She waited to have any more kids until she married a few years ago."

"When you were in middle school?" I asked, thinking about the change we saw in Eddie around that time.

"Yeah." He frowned a little finding my comment strange. Then he looked at Suzy and smiled again. "I'm taking care of them during the summer. Mom takes on two shifts during the summer while I watch the kids. Then she goes back to work only evenings when I'm in school."

"Who takes care of the kids in the evenings? Their dad?" I asked. When I didn't get an answer, I looked up to find Eddie shift from one foot to the other. I knew the answer. He did. He was in charge of all of these kids every day when he got home.

"He took off when Mom was pregnant with Gabe. So it's just my mom and me."

"Oh, that explains it." I said before I could think about my words.

"Explains what?" Eddie was defensive.

I smiled at him. "Your comment at the lunch table."

Eddie relaxed. "Oh, that."

"Neema!" Romero yelled down the aisle. "Need you at register two."

"Coming!" I yelled back. I looked at Eddie. "Listen Eddie. You stick with your brothers and sister. They look good on you." I smiled. A huge smile crossed Eddie's face.

I don't know why I said it. There was something about Eddie that made me want to be nice to him. Maybe I'd felt guilty for laughing at him.

CHAPTER 30

Week 34

Baby's sitting right," Dr. Baker's voice said as he pressed on my belly. "Her head's down."

"That's a good thing, right?" I asked, feeling stupid. Mom and Aunt Amina were sitting in the waiting room since we weren't going to have an ultrasound. It would be like all the other appointments. Weight, blood pressure, heartbeat, and measuring my stomach.

Dr. Baker smiled at me. "That's a good thing. You want her head to come out first." He paused and then looked at me. I could tell he was trying to be nice. "Miss Powell, have you not been reading about your pregnancy at all?"

I frowned and shook my head like a girl who hadn't done her homework. "I didn't really think I needed to. Don't you tell me everything?"

Dr. Baker pulled up his small stool and sat next to me. "Yes, I tell you much of what you need to know. But there is so much more. Have you gone to any of the classes to prepare you for the birth? Or breastfeeding?"

I sort of remembered Dr. Baker handing us a schedule with dates and times for certain classes. I had put them on my dresser and never looked at them again. "I thought they were suggestions, not something I had to do."

"Miss Powell, I can't force you to learn about what's happening to your body or what to expect during birth. But most women want to know."

He wasn't fussing at me. But I still felt like a stupid child. Then I was suddenly angry with Aunt Amina and Mom. They should have made me go.

"Will she not be born right since I missed the classes?" I asked.

Dr. Baker laughed. "Trust me. The baby will come out the way millions of other babies have. She will be just fine." He paused. "It's you, though. I want you to be ready in your mind about what you're going to go through."

"You're scaring me, Dr. Baker!" I started to think about all I was facing. "My baby could be born any time in the next month. And I'm starting my senior year tomorrow. Now I find out I really don't know what I'm doing."

Dr. Baker stood up and walked up to me. He patted my leg. "Miss Powell, you have a lot on your plate. I don't mean to scare you. You'll do fine. I'm sure of it." He tried to sound like he meant it, but I could tell he was ready to end the discussion.

Aunt Amina and Mom walked on each side of me to the subway. "What's wrong?" Aunt Amina asked.

"Why didn't you make me go to those classes where I learn about what I'm going to go through during birth?" I was angry and didn't hold back.

Aunt Amina took my arm and made me stop walking. "Listen here! Don't you blame this on us. We didn't get pregnant!" A few strangers glanced our way. I didn't pay them any attention. I didn't care what anyone thought anymore.

"Amina!" Mom spoke, but Aunt Amina gave her a shut-up look.

Aunt Amina continued. "We are here for you, Neema, but this is your body and your baby!" She took a deep breath. "This is the first we've heard from you that you want to know what it's like to give birth." She let go of my arm and started walking again. She added one more thing. "You want to learn about giving birth? Then you'll learn about it!"

The next night and for the whole next week Aunt Amina brought home books and DVDs from the library. By the time she was done with me, I wished I hadn't said anything. I watched women scream while they gave birth. I watched a slimy baby being wiped off while his cord was cut. I saw white babies, black babies, Asian babies, and Hispanic babies. They all looked the same. Wrinkled with eyes closed and heads all funny shaped. Yes, I wished I hadn't said anything. After that I was really scared.

CHAPTER 31

Back to School

The year started strangely. The fact that I spent the evenings of my whole first week of school watching birthing DVDs didn't help any. I thought I'd feel relieved that Nate had graduated. I didn't have to worry about seeing him at all. But part of me kept hoping he'd say something to me about the baby. *Anything.* Once in a while I saw Bella. She looked a little lost. I didn't want to ask, but I guessed she'd been dumped too.

"Hey, coming to the party tonight?" Rose slid up to me in the hall. I couldn't help but notice Mike right behind her. He put his arm on her shoulder.

I frowned just a little. "What's that?" I pointed at their closeness.

Rose smiled. "I finally caught Mike."

"I don't know who caught who since I've been after you for years." Mike kissed her cheek. It made my insides turn. I wasn't sure why. Maybe Mike had always been safe. He was never one of the guys who were out for one thing. He was a friend.

Rose poked me with a frown. "Aren't you happy for us?"

I pulled myself together. "Yeah. Sure. It's just weird." I couldn't help but share what was on my mind. "I had no idea; that's all." I smiled and gave the two of them a hug. My stomach felt like a huge basketball between us. "I am happy for you." Then I spoke without thinking. "Just remember to use your birth control the right way."

"Neema!" Rose looked embarrassed. Mike was laughing his head off. It was obvious they hadn't gotten that far yet.

"Sorry." I patted my belly. "It's kind of on my mind!" I felt the baby kick. I smiled and kept touching the little lump that was her foot that was pushing from the inside.

Mike reached out to touch my belly. This time he could feel the motion. His touch didn't feel strange this time. He was, after all, only a friend. Rose joined in. "Feels like she's going to push her way out."

"That's how it works, isn't it?" Mike teased.

"Shut up, Mr. Know-It-All!" Rose slapped his arm. I guess I'd never paid attention to their teasing through the years. They had flirted like third graders for a long time.

Rose looked at him again. "So, coming to the party?"

"After work." I smiled.

I left Rose and Mike and walked toward my first period

class. I turned the corner and found myself face to face with Eddie. "Hey, Eddie." I smiled. A bunch of girls stopped to look at me. They probably wondered why I was even talking to him. He'd pretty much ticked off most of the girls in school.

He smiled. But it was almost shy. Not normal for sleazy Eddie. "Hey, Neema."

"How's Suzy?" I asked as Eddie started to walk next to me.

"She's fine. It's the boys I worry about. They all have a cold and can't seem to get rid of it."

I thought for a moment. "You know, if it doesn't get better, I saw Romero put some of the cold medicine on sale. I work tomorrow, so I could show you where it is." Eddie stopped and looked at me strangely. I gave him a hard stare. "Now don't go weird on me, Eddie. This is *not* a date!"

He laughed. It was a real laugh. Then he got serious. Before I turned to walk into my classroom, he whispered, "Thanks, Neema."

CHAPTER 32

Saturday, September 10

I was tired. The first week of school had been a lot. I realized I really didn't want to go to Tia's party that evening. I knew I would be even more tired after work. I usually liked heading into the Big Save, but my stomach was bothering me. I hoped I wasn't coming down with the flu.

"Neema, you're late." Romero teased as I walked in thirty minutes late.

I pointed at my belly, using it as an excuse. "Do you want me to tell you how often I used the toilet this morning?" I hollered back. He laughed and waved me on.

I stood for two hours pouring as much kindness onto our customers as I was able to. My stomach felt really strange. It started tightening. I would bend over for a minute and then it would go away. "I really don't need the flu right now," I told myself.

"Are you okay?" Romero came up behind me.

I quickly stood back up. "Yes, just really tired." I didn't want him to think I was passing flu germs on to our customers.

The stomach pains started coming in longer waves, and my stomach felt like a hard rock. Then it would go away. I kept telling myself I couldn't be in labor. Not yet. I still had two weeks to go. After an hour of this I could no longer stand up straight even if I tried. I suddenly knew this was the real thing.

"Romero!" I yelled. He ran over to me.

"Neema, what's wrong?" He looked pale.

"What do you think?" I barely got the words out before my stomach tightened like a rock again. Pain shot through my back like something was taking over my body.

"Neema?" Eddie's voice came up next to me. He must have shown up for the cold medicine.

"Eddie?" I tried to stand up straight. I could see he was worried. "Looks like the little girl is on her way." I tried to smile, but pain made me buckle over again.

"Let's call nine-one-one." Romero was panicking. I could feel customers watching us but trying to go about their business.

"Wait!" Eddie said. Romero paused, ready to listen to the tall, young black man. "Have you timed the contractions?"

I shook my head.

"What difference does that make? Let's call nine-one-one." Romero was pulling out his cell.

"Please listen!" Eddie spoke softly but firmly. "It could take hours before the baby comes. If she's only beginning then she needs to move around." He looked at his watch. "Let's time the contractions first. If they are under three minutes apart, then you call nine-one-one. If not, then you let me deal with her." I found it strange to listen to the deal being made between the two men.

"Fine!" Romero stood there with his phone open.

The pain finally stopped. It was strange. It was almost like a memory. One that I couldn't believe would ever repeat itself.

We waited. I could breathe easy. "So, Eddie, where are the kids?" I asked, feeling strange waiting around with two men watching me like I was a freak show.

"They're at home with Mom. She's not working today. I thought I'd take you up on that cold medicine." He smiled.

We chatted a few minutes before the wave of pain possessed me again.

"How long?" Romero asked.

"Six minutes," Eddie stated.

"Now what?" Romero frowned.

I felt myself holding back a scream. I wanted to yell at the two men. I wanted to get to the hospital. I didn't care what they thought.

As I pulled out of the wave of pain, I welcomed the peace that relaxed my body.

Eddie spoke directly to me like I was a child he had to command. "Neema, you need to walk with me. We'll walk to the hospital."

"Walk?" I was almost yelling. "That's five blocks!" I shook my head.

"Trust me, Neema!" Eddie took my hand. He had my purse around his shoulder. Romero must have given it to him. His hand felt strong and warm. Not clammy. Not sweaty. Eddie continued to explain. "If you walk for the first part, it will give you less time to spend in the hospital halls. Trust me. Mom always waited until she was under five minutes before she headed to the hospital. It can take hours. Like ten or twelve or more."

"Great!" I said with misery. I picked up my phone and called Mom. There was no answer, so I left a message telling her I was in labor. Then I followed Eddie out into the busy parking lot. Instead of heading to the subway, he led me down Fifth Street. I knew Park Mission Hospital was down this street, and I knew we'd planned to use it when the time came. But I never imagined walking there with Eddie Franklin. At least the hot summer sun was no longer around. It was warm, but I didn't have the need to fling my clothes off of me.

My phone rang and I picked up. "Neema, are you

okay?" Mom's voice made me relax. I told her I was with Eddie, and we'd meet her at the hospital. She didn't know who Eddie was, so that didn't help any. "What are you doing walking five blocks to the hospital with a strange boy?" I couldn't believe she was fussing at me.

"It's not like we're going to have sex or anything!" I yelled back. Eddie laughed. I couldn't handle any fussing. I felt a wave of pain flood across my body. I grabbed the side of the building and handed the phone to Eddie. "You talk to her."

I heard Eddie say, yes, ma'am, and no, ma'am, a few times before he hung up. It didn't upset him at all. He looked at me and spoke softly. "Breathe, Neema. In and out. Your mom and aunt are on their way." He started breathing like he wanted me to. I followed his lead. It helped some. Made me feel I was doing something. Anything to participate in this physical takeover. He looked at his watch again. He was good at sounding calm. "Okay, so we're at five minutes now."

"There's no we," I panted. "Doesn't that mean they're coming faster?"

He smiled. "Yes, they are! Let's keep walking."

I tried to keep up with Eddie. He was walking without worry. "It's a show isn't it?" I finally asked. I wanted to talk about something besides the next contraction.

"What is?" He turned his head to look at me as I waddled next to him.

"Your sleazy self," I said without trying to be mean.

He lifted his eyebrows, "Me, sleazy?" He laughed. "Never." Then he pretended to be hurt.

"Come on, Eddie." I gently punched his arm. "When you're not at school, you're ... different."

"I'll take that as a compliment." He did a silly bow.

"Why?" I asked.

I could see him get serious. "Better to be a jerk no one wants than a guy no one can have.

I thought for a moment. "The kids?"

He nodded. "Yes, I've had to help Mom for as long as I can remember. I can't let everyone know I take care of babies. Not really a manly trait."

"I disagree." I smiled. His eyes met mine and for the first time I found myself flirting with Eddie.

"Are you hitting on me, Neema?" Eddie laughed.

"Weird, huh?" I patted my belly as I waddled down the street. "Perfect timing to hit on a guy." We both laughed. The next wave of pain took over. The brief moment of flirtation was gone.

But Eddie Franklin was not. He stuck with me and walked me all the way to the hospital. By the time we reached the waiting room, I was having contractions every three minutes.

CHAPTER 33

Birth

Eddie didn't leave me until Aunt Amina and Mom showed up. They thanked him, and he turned to go. I could tell he wanted to stay. I wanted him to stay. "Eddie," I started as the nurse was ready to show me my room.

"See you around!" Eddie brushed me off. He wouldn't let me ask him to stay. It would be too close, too fast. Then he smiled. "Don't forget to breathe."

I smiled back. "I won't."

After another three hours of painful contractions, the doctors finally gave me a shot in my back. I welcomed the medicine that made it so I couldn't feel my lower body. It felt strange watching my stomach tighten but not feeling the pain.

As the afternoon turned into evening, the doctor told me I was making little progress. I needed to stop the medicine so I could push. I wasn't happy about the flood of pain returning. I gave in to screams and cursing. No one fussed at me. Mom and Aunt Amina squeezed my hands as I pushed with all my strength. Then everything would stop. I was so tired. I thought I could sleep. But only seconds later the next wave of pain pulled me back.

About an hour after I had started pushing the doctor said, "Neema, if you push as hard as you can this could be your last one." Last one? That's all I needed to hear. I pushed. I focused every last inch of my energy on the push.

Suddenly there was a strange feeling that moved through me. I was suddenly no longer holding a life inside of me. My stomach was still big, but a small mass was placed on top of me. It took me a moment to realize it was my baby. Black hair pressed against her funny-shaped head. Small fingers and toes wiggled around. The doctor was busy cutting the cord as I reached out to touch the slimy baby. My slimy baby.

CHAPTER 34

Name

What's your baby's name?" the nurse asked as she handed me the cleaned-up bundle. I held the little fingers and watched the baby try to open her eyes. I looked at Mom and Aunt Amina. They'd given me their list of names. I didn't like any of them. I guess part of me wanted to see her first. A flood of tears fell. I panicked and couldn't believe the baby was mine. I couldn't raise a child. I couldn't figure this out. Then from somewhere deep I heard the words from *I Know Why the Caged Bird Sings*: "See, you don't have to think about doing the right thing. If you're for the right thing, then you do it without thinking."

"Maya," I suddenly said. That would be her name. Maya Angelou had given me strength. I would speak Maya's name and draw the strength I needed to be a mother. I would have to find out what the right thing was. But I was sure I could do it.

Mom and Aunt Amina looked at me and smiled. Aunt Amina kissed the little fingers and said, "Hi, little Maya."

Mom kissed my head. "Great name, Neema. Great name."

CHAPTER 35

Postpartum

Sore. I was sore and tired. I was thankful Mom and Aunt Amina were around. They spent the first two days holding the baby and bringing her to me so I could nurse her. My nipples felt like knives were slicing them apart. "It'll feel better after a few days," Mom whispered after she took Maya from me and let me fall back to sleep. I searched for the strength I'd felt in the hospital. But it was gone. All I wanted to do was sleep.

I remembered Tia, Rose, and Mike coming over, but I couldn't get out of bed. They laughed and said Maya was beautiful, but that's all I remember. I didn't care. They didn't stay long.

I could feel my world slipping away. I had never felt so lost, so out of control, so trapped. I had a baby that I couldn't turn off when I needed to sleep. Every two hours I was jarred awake. Then there was school. I still had a whole year ahead of me. How could I do it when all I wanted to do was sleep? The more sleep I got, the more sleep I wanted.

"You need to get up." After one week Aunt Amina had finally had enough. "You need to love on your baby not just feed her."

I pulled myself up and threw on some sweatpants. My belly was still stretched out, and I was wearing large, very large, pads to catch all the blood that still had to work its way out of my body.

I sat down on the couch, and Mom placed Maya in my lap. I held her and saw her small eyes were wide and open. She was looking at me and reaching for my breast. "I don't know what to do." I felt sort of stupid.

"You don't have to do anything," Mom said. "Just touch her and love her."

A feeling swept across me, and I started crying again. "I can't do this. I thought I could, but I can't." I started to hand the baby back to Mom, but she didn't take her. I was left looking down at this baby that didn't feel like mine. I sat there and cried. I didn't see how I could go to school, have friends, have a boyfriend, work, and raise a baby. I felt so tired. Aunt Amina came over and took Maya from me. "You go back to bed. I'll call Dr. Baker."

I didn't care what she did. I went back to bed.

The next day Aunt Amina and Mom cleaned me up enough to walk me into Dr. Baker's office. They explained how I'd been sleeping all the time. That I seemed to not care about anything including the baby.

Dr. Baker walked over to me and spoke softly, "So you're quite depressed?"

I frowned. "I don't know what it is." I started to cry again. I hated myself. I felt like a child and out of control.

"Miss Powell, listen to me." Dr. Baker's voice pulled me away from my pity party. I looked at him. "This is common for some women. They experience postpartum depression."

"What?" I asked not sure what he'd just said.

"That means your hormones are so out of whack you become really depressed." He walked over to the small table in the room and grabbed a pad of paper. "I'm going to give you some medicine to help you." He started to write.

"What about the baby?" Aunt Amina asked. "She's nursing."

"How is your nursing going?" Dr. Baker seemed to ignore Aunt Amina's question.

"I'm having a hard time." I told him my nipples were still very sore.

"Are you going back to school soon?" he asked. I nodded, not knowing when that would be. "Then I suggest you stop nursing, and let your body adjust before you go back to school. That way you won't worry about the medicine getting into your baby's bloodstream."

"But it's best for the baby if she nurses!" Aunt Amina argued.

Dr. Baker smiled at her. "Yes, it is. Neema has done a great job so far giving the baby some very important nutrients. However," he paused, "what's best for the baby right now is Neema getting better." Aunt Amina looked at me. I looked awful. She just nodded.

I didn't know if Dr. Baker was just trying to give me permission to stop breastfeeding. But it helped me feel less guilty for wanting to stop.

He handed me the sheet of paper with the prescription on it. "You'll feel better within days, maybe even hours," he paused, adding, "But in a few months we'll start getting you off the medicine. You won't need it anymore."

I was surprised it only took a couple of days. I woke up Monday morning and heard Maya crying. She'd been sleeping in the living room with my mother. Something clicked inside of me. I went into the kitchen and warmed a bottle of formula. I pulled Maya up into my arms and sat in the overstuffed chair.

I watched the baby suck and coo. I could still feel my breasts fill up with milk. I suddenly ached to let Maya relieve my pain. Not breastfeeding suddenly was more painful than I thought it would be. I smiled at my longing to feed my baby. Maybe I wasn't such a bad mother after all. It wouldn't be long before I would stop making my own milk. I told myself that was a good thing. I would need to go back to school soon. Pumping milk from my breasts between classes would not work at my school. I told myself I had made the best decision. I rocked and saw Maya gurgle. I smiled back. I'd made my baby happy.

I looked up at my mother who was still lying on the couch with her eyes open. She had a huge grin on her face. "She'll sleep in my room from now on," I stated.

Mom smiled. "It's about time."

CHAPTER 36

Phone Call

I don't know what got into me. Maya was two weeks old. I hadn't thought about Nate much. But, holding our baby brought back a flood of memories. I took Maya with me into the bedroom and gently placed her on the quilt that still covered my bed. I sat down next to her as I pulled out my phone. I stared at his number for a few minutes. I still had it saved under my contacts. I thought I had pushed Nate out of my life. The fact that I still had his number made me realize I'd lied to myself.

My heart raced as I pushed send. I wasn't sure he'd even answer.

"Neema?" His voice almost surprised me. I expected to get his voice mail.

"Hi, Nate." I paused for a moment. There was silence on the other end. I was sure he was waiting for me to tell him the news. I spoke as softly as I could, "I gave birth to a beautiful baby girl two weeks ago. I named her Maya."

There was still silence. But he didn't hang up. So I continued. "I thought you might want to know."

He finally spoke, "Thanks."

I suddenly couldn't take it. Thanks isn't the reply anyone should give after hearing their child has been born. I tried to keep calm, but it was hard. "Come on, Nate. She's your baby. Aren't you in the least bit interested?"

"Neema!" Nate's voice didn't hide his own frustration. "What do you want from me?"

It was my turn to be silent. I had to think. I finally answered, "I guess I want you to be Maya's father. Whatever that looks like." It was the most honest answer I could give.

"I can't!" He spoke as if he were suddenly in a hurry. Someone called his name. It was some girl. Some new girl in his life. He quickly whispered, "I can't. Not now. I'm not ready."

"I wasn't ready either, Nate," I answered. "I'm still not ready. But I don't have a choice. She's mine. Ours."

"You did have a choice. You still do have choices." Nate was trying to sound like he knew what he was talking about. But he didn't have a clue. He yelled to the voice that he was coming.

My stomach suddenly hurt. "Are you saying I should've had an abortion? Or that I should give up my baby?" I was getting angry now.

"No, Neema." Nate was getting ticked. "I'm saying you have to live with your choices, and I have to live with mine." He paused. "Don't call me again."

"I won't." I hung up and cried. He didn't want to have anything to do with Maya. I snuggled up next to Maya pulling the quilt over both of us. She was mine. Only mine.

CHAPTER 37

Back in the World

The school had sent me work, and I had done my best to keep up with it. That is, after I was back to feeling like myself. It was hard to do the work without a teacher. But I did what I could. I had only missed three weeks of school. During the third week, I asked Mike to help me when it was too hard. He came by a few times, and I was thankful.

When Maya was four weeks old, I was starting to get into a pattern. Rose and Tia dared to come back and see me. Everyone loved little Maya. Even Romero came by with a huge basket of groceries and diapers. He loved on the baby and then fussed at me for leaving him shorthanded at work. I told him he'd get over it.

But I had not seen Eddie. I pushed the thought away. Why would he come by? He didn't even know where I lived. He didn't even have my number.

"So when are you coming back?" Tia was holding the small baby blanket as Rose rocked the baby.

"The doctor said I could head back as soon as I felt like I was up for it." I paused and thought a moment. "I might try next week."

"Great!" Rose handed Tia the baby so she could have a turn. "We miss you. It will be fun to have you back."

"Hey, Neema." Tia's eyes grew wide. "Next weekend we're having a party at my house. It could be a party for you!"

I smiled. "When will it be?"

"Saturday night." She grinned.

I frowned. "What about Maya?"

Tia kissed the baby's head. "Why don't you bring her along? It would be a perfect way to show her off."

I didn't quite understand why I didn't get excited. Since I couldn't explain it, I pushed the feeling away. I had told Romero that I wouldn't be back to work for six weeks. This meant I wouldn't be too tired to go to a party. That's what I told myself. I finally said, "Okay."

I spent the rest of the week finishing my school work and trying on my old clothes to see what would fit. My stomach was finally going down some, but my breasts were still huge.

We came up with a plan. Mom would watch Maya until two every day. Then she would go to work. Aunt Amina would watch Maya from two until I got home. This meant she took a very late two-hour lunch break before she headed back to the library. Then it was my turn. Maya was my responsibility for any other part of the day. It seemed like it would work. At least I could go to school.

The first couple of days of school were hard. I wanted to sleep. I was still getting up to give Maya a bottle every two or three hours at night. I was in the habit of sleeping when Maya slept. Suddenly, I couldn't nap anymore. Rose, Tia, and Mike kept waking me up when I would nod off. Mom and Aunt Amina agreed to take turns and take one feeding at night. I still had to take care of the rest of Maya's nighttime needs. That helped some. By Friday of that first week back I was feeling better. I could do this.

"Where's Eddie?" I finally asked Rose after a whole week of not running into him. We were sitting next to each other in senior English.

"Why do you care?" Rose was a little too disgusted with Eddie.

"He did help me when I was in labor," I stated. "I should thank him."

Rose sighed. "I guess so." She rolled her eyes, "That was just weird though. I mean Eddie Franklin? Are you sure that was him? Maybe you were just imagining things?"

"Shut up, Rose," I tried to say it gently, but my frustration showed.

She leaned on her desk and stared at me. "No! Don't tell!" She started to laugh. "Are you falling for him?"

I shook my head. "No, Rose. You don't know him. It's just ..."

Rose was laughing so hard I thought she'd pee on herself.

"Rose!" I reached out and grabbed her arm. "It's not like that. I just can't figure out why I haven't seen him."

She wiped her eyes. "Don't know why you haven't. I've seen him all over the building. He's still hitting on every girl he can." She patted my hand gently trying not to laugh. "I guess now that you're a momma you're no longer in his line of vision." Then she whispered in my ear, "But if you really like him, we'll have to change his point of view."

Rose was having fun with me, but her statement bothered me. I didn't want her to be right. But what if she was? Was he really not interested in me? Was everything we talked about really nothing? Or was he avoiding me?

I walked out of my English class into the hall. I dreaded Saturday night. I didn't really want to bring Maya. I would feel like a freak show. But I had promised Rose and Tia I would come. I really wanted life to get back to normal.

"Hey, Eddie!" Rose yelled down the hall. I turned around to find Rose about ten feet away from me. She looked at me as I ran up to her. I saw Eddie at the end of the hall, heading for a group of girls.

"What are you doing?" I asked.

She smiled and winked at me, "Watch this," she whispered. Then she waved at Eddie. "Eddie, come here."

Eddie looked at Rose and back at the girls who were telling him to go away. Then I saw him glance at me. His eyes dropped and then came quickly back up with a fake smile for Rose. He walked in what he thought was a cool step. "Hey, Rose. You need me now? After all these years?"

"Shut up, Eddie." She looked at me and then back at Eddie. "Neema's been looking for you."

He let his eyes find mine. He didn't say anything. We just stared at each other. What could I say? How did he want me to act? Rose broke into our silence. "So why don't you come to Neema's party at Tia's house tomorrow night?"

"I can't," Eddie said almost before she'd finished asking.

"What?" Rose frowned. "You've been dying for people to invite you to parties and no one ever does. Now you're invited, and you won't come?" Rose tried one more time. "Neema's bringing her baby."

I dropped my eyes. I wasn't happy that Eddie knew I was bringing Maya. He'd protected his brothers and sister from the party life, and I was already introducing it to a five-week-old.

"I'll see what I can do." Eddie had his fake smile on. "See ya around." He waved and headed back down the hall.

"Thanks, Rose!" I said, not hiding my frustration.

"Oh, come on, Neema! It'll be fun." Rose kept smiling. It was one big game to her. "If he likes you, he'll show up. If not, then you can move on."

CHAPTER 38

Stupid

Are you stupid?" Aunt Amina was angry. She placed a pan on the stove top with a little too much force. Mom was sitting on the couch shaking her head.

"Don't call me stupid!" I started to raise my voice. I shoved a bottle of formula in the baby's diaper bag.

"Think about it, Neema." She was not holding back, "Taking a five-week-old to Tia's house on a Saturday night sounds stupid. There will probably be other people showing up. Regardless of what you tell me, I can smell a party a mile away." She turned to grab a can of beans from the counter.

Aunt Amina was saying what I was feeling. But I couldn't back down. She was making me angry. "It's Saturday. I'll still meet my ten o'clock curfew if that's what you're worried about!"

"Neema." Mom stood up and came in closer. "You're a mother now. You can't run around to parties anymore." She paused. "Maya is not your sister that Amina and I are going to raise while you're out doing your thing. She's your child."

I felt cornered. I held Maya close. "That's why she's coming with me!"

"Neema!" Mom and Aunt Amina yelled as I walked out the door.

They were right. I knew they were right. But I didn't want them to make all my decisions for me. I wanted to figure some things out on my own.

CHAPTER 39

Party

Hey, Neema! Look at that sweet baby!" A girl I hardly knew wanted to hold Maya. I didn't want her to, but she took Maya out of my arms and a small group of girls started passing the baby around. I couldn't believe I was at the party. Dumb.

"Neema!" Tia yelled. She grabbed the baby from the small crowd of girls. "Maya is so cute! You make me want to go out and have a baby!" Tia giggled.

"No, Tia!" I tried to yell over the growing loudness of music as we walked into the small living room. It was standing room only. Maya started to fuss. I tried to reach for her when Rose came by and grabbed her. She held her as she walked into the kitchen. I followed them. I ran into a couple that was kissing. "A little early don't you think?" Rose teased the girl who giggled and pulled her man into a back room. Tia ran after them, pulling them back out into the living room.

The smell of alcohol seemed stronger than usual. "What are you drinking?" I asked Rose as she lifted a plastic cup to her lips.

"Vodka," she giggled. "I think."

I reached for Maya and took her with force. She started crying. "Look what you've done," Rose fussed. "Maybe Maya would settle down with a finger tip of my drink?"

"Stop it, Rose! Maya is *not* a doll!" I yelled.

"Rose!" Mike's voice came up behind me. He must have just showed up at the party. "What are you doing?"

Rose smiled at her man as he walked over to her. "Having some fun." She held a plastic cup up to him. "Come on and have some fun too."

Mike frowned. "Stop it." He pushed her hand away.

Rose pouted, "Please, Mike. Maybe tonight is the night." She gently touched his chest.

Mike took her hand and held it. "Not when you've been drinking!" Then he looked at me and Maya. "Neema, what are you doing here? Why did you bring Maya? This is no place for her. Are you nuts?"

"Sure it is." Rose held up her plastic cup to me. I let it hang in mid-air. Tia walked up and took in the scene. She took the cup from Rose.

I looked at Rose and Mike and said, "I'm going to the bathroom." I held Maya tightly as I hurried into the small bathroom. I took a deep breath and looked into the mirror. I didn't see the sexy Neema looking for a good time. I saw a mother with a baby. A mother who didn't know what she was doing. A mother who wished she'd stayed at home snuggled under her quilt. I looked down at the sink. The rusty circles reminded me I was still at Tia's house. I still had to face my friends. I took one more deep breath and kissed the top of Maya's head. Her baby smell swept over me, filling my body with renewed energy.

I stepped into the hall. I walked back down to the kitchen. I found my friends and smiled. "I'm going home."

Rose looked at me and tried to smile. "I know Maya is not a toy."

"We know that, Neema." Tia came between us. "You need to relax. We love Maya. We would never hurt her. We're going to have so much fun with her."

Tia hadn't even been drinking much, yet her words jolted through my body like a cold shower. I'd changed. My friendships with Tia and Rose would have to change.

I knew what was right. This party was not right. "I'll see you at school," I said calmly as I left my friends behind. I quickly pushed my way through the bodies in the living room. They didn't even see me.

"Neema," Mike's voice followed me outside. I looked at him and was about to say something, but he spoke first. "You're doing the right thing." He smiled.

"You're a good friend, you know." I smiled. "But you have your hands full with Rose."

Mike nodded. "Yeah, I know." Then he looked back at the lights coming from the windows. "But there's something about her ... when she's not drinking."

I shook my head. "Good luck!" We both laughed.

I watched him head back to the party. I felt very alone. I found myself suddenly hurrying down the street. I wasn't really sad. I was awake. I had made a choice that made me feel free. I didn't have to stick with my old life. It didn't work anymore. I suddenly knew I had to take care of Maya. I had to take care of me. I had to do it right the first time. Only then would she make better choices. Choices she could be proud of.

CHAPTER 40

Strong

"Where are you going?" Eddie's voice slowed me down. I had almost run past him. He was sitting on a bench.

"Eddie?" I wiped my face. "What are you doing here? I thought you couldn't come."

"Mom had the night off, so I thought I'd head to the only party I've ever been invited to." He smiled. "But I decided I'd rather be alone. Then you came along."

I pulled Maya up on my shoulder. She had stopped fussing since the music wasn't blasting. Eddie suddenly stood. He walked in close. He started to reach out but stopped. "May I?"

I nodded and watched him gently take Maya in his large hands. He knew what he was doing. He got down close to her and whispered words I didn't understand. Maya looked up at him and was reaching for his nose. He smiled at me. "She's beautiful."

I smiled back. "I know." He sat back down on the bench

with Maya resting on his legs. I sat down next to him and put the diaper bag down.

"Why aren't you at the party?" he asked.

"No place for a baby." I tried to smile, but Eddie could see through me. He knew it was more than that. Something had changed. "So do you have any tips?"

Eddie looked away from me to keep playing with the baby. "You mean like when she gets sick or how to deal with crying?"

I laughed. "No, I have my aunt and mom for that." I paused, thinking about the two women waiting at home for me, worrying—two women who were eager to help me. I looked at Eddie. "I mean tips for how to reinvent yourself."

Eddie looked up. He dropped his smile. "I don't think I'm the right person to ask that," he sighed. "It's only turned me into someone on the outside that I really don't want to be."

I gently shoved his shoulder. "I think that's better than pretending to be someone nice, but the real you is the creep." He looked at me and smiled.

"So what now?" Eddie handed me the baby. Our hands touched. He moved slowly away.

"What if you just act like who you really are?" I was serious. "The girls will love you and will really love your brothers and sister."

"I don't want *all* the girls to love me." His eyes shot straight into me.

I knew he was hinting. I knew he wanted me to fall for him. Part of me wanted to, but a stronger part of me held back. "Eddie, I need time," I whispered. "If I fall into another relationship right now, I might not find out a few things."

Eddie sat up straight. He'd opened himself up to me, and I wasn't jumping in. "Like what?" He tried to sound relaxed, but I could tell he was hurt.

"Like how to do the right thing? How I can be a good mom? I have so much to learn," I paused. I looked at him. He didn't look back at first, but he finally did. "Then there's the big question."

"What's that?"

"Can I learn to have a guy as a friend? I mean really get to know him. Really find out who he is before he becomes my boyfriend?" I kept Eddie's focus. His eyes changed. He didn't look hurt anymore. I think he got it.

He reached out and took my hand and smiled. "Can I be your first victim?"

I laughed and squeezed his hand and then let go. "Maybe."

We sat and talked for another half hour before we parted. Both of us were smiling.

When I finally headed home, I felt strong. Strong because I was not the same girl I'd been ten months ago.

Strong because I didn't need to have a man to be somebody. Strong because I was learning what a real friend was. Strong because I had two amazing women to guide me. Strong because I had hopes for Maya. She didn't have to be me or my mom. She could have so much more. I would be there for her. Strong.

Want to Keep Reading?...

Turn the page for a sneak peek at another book from the Gravel Road series: M.G. Higgins' *I'm Just Me*.

ISBN: 978-1-62250-721-4

CHAPTER 1

Nasreen

I knock on my brother's door. His rap music is so loud, I'm sure he can't hear me. I pound louder. "Jaffar! Open up!"

The volume goes down. He opens his door a crack and glares at me. "What?"

I clear my throat. He never lets me forget that he's older than me. That I'm just his little sister. "I need your help," I say.

He glances at the pamphlets I'm holding. "College brochures? You're only a junior."

"I know. I'm starting early."

He rolls his eyes. "Of course you are."

"I don't have a clue where to go or how to apply."

"Okay." He sighs. "Come in." He takes the pamphlets from me. Shakes his head as he glances at the first cover. "Harvard? No way."

"Why not?"

He fingers through the rest. "Cal Tech? MIT? Stanford? Nasreen, these are all top universities."

"So?"

"So our parents aren't rich."

"Mr. Clarke said I can apply for scholarships."

"I applied for scholarships and where am I going?"

"But you want to be an accountant. State college is perfect for you."

"Oh, that's right," he says. "You're the brains in the family." He shoves the brochures back at me.

"I just want your advice."

"And who advised me? No one. Because I'm the oldest and did it myself. Go online and figure it out." He turns his music up.

I leave, closing the door behind me.

Back in my bedroom, I set the brochures on my desk. I think about asking my parents. But they know nothing about American colleges. As I sink into my beanbag chair, I imagine all the kids at school whose parents will be helping them decide which colleges to apply to. Parents who aren't from Pakistan and get confused by American rules and language.

Taking a deep breath, I pull my calculus book onto my lap. I enter a few numbers into my graphing calculator and try to ignore Jaffar's loud music thumping through our shared wall.

By ten o'clock, my homework is finished. I wish I had more. I start thinking about school tomorrow. The familiar knot ties in my stomach.

Mom pokes her head around my door. "It's time for bed, Nasreen," she says in Punjabi.

"I know," I mutter back in English.

"What's wrong?"

"Nothing."

She stares at me a moment. Then she says, "Good night," closing my door.

My parents have a hard enough time just getting by in this country. I decided a long time ago I wouldn't be one of the things they had to worry about. Just a year and a half. A year and a half and I won't have to deal with the students at Arondale High School anymore.

It's a little too early when I get to the bus stop. I lean against a tree, away from the others, trying to make myself invisible. When the bus pulls up, I stand at the back of the crowd, my jaw tight, my eyes lowered. Guys jostle and shove each other as they get on.

We're one of the first stops. That's good because I can always find an empty seat. Not so good because it's twenty more minutes until we get to school.

The bus starts moving. From the back seat, Samantha shouts, "Hey, I just figured out why she wears that stupid scarf!"

"Why?" her friend Melody asks, setting her up.

"To protect her head from bird poop. I wish *I* had one."

They laugh.

The bus driver glares at them in the rearview mirror and shakes her head. Samantha and her friends won't say anything else, or they'll get written up. I shrink into my seat anyway. At the next stop, Kyle Spencer sits behind me. My shoulders rise protectively around my neck.

"Hi, Nasty Nasreen," he whispers through my *hijab*. I lean away from him, curling my fingers into fists. I review math equations in my head.

At the next stop, someone sits next to me. No one *ever* shares my seat. Great. What do I have to put up with now?